HELL'S KITCHEN

CULLEN & BAIN 3

ED JAMES

Copyright © 2020 Ed James

The right of Ed James to be identified as the author of this work has been asserted in accordance with the Copyright, Designs and Patents Act 1988. All rights reserved.

No part of this publication may be reproduced, stored in or transmitted into any retrieval system, in any form, or by any means (electronic, mechanical, photocopying, recording or otherwise) without the prior written permission of the publisher. Any person who does any unauthorised act in relation to this publication may be liable to criminal prosecution and civil claims for damages.

This is a work of fiction. Names, characters, businesses, places, events and incidents are either the products of the author's imagination or used in a fictitious manner. Any resemblance to actual persons, living or dead, or actual events is purely coincidental.

Cover design copyright © Ed James

OTHER BOOKS BY ED JAMES

SCOTT CULLEN MYSTERIES SERIES

1. GHOST IN THE MACHINE
2. DEVIL IN THE DETAIL
3. FIRE IN THE BLOOD
4. STAB IN THE DARK
5. COPS & ROBBERS
6. LIARS & THIEVES
7. COWBOYS & INDIANS
8. HEROES & VILLAINS

CULLEN & BAIN SERIES

1. CITY OF THE DEAD
2. WORLD'S END
3. HELL'S KITCHEN
4. GORE GLEN (November 2020)

CRAIG HUNTER SERIES

1. MISSING
2. HUNTED
3. THE BLACK ISLE

DS VICKY DODDS

1. TOOTH & CLAW
2. FLESH & BLOOD
3. SKIN & BONE (May 2021)

DI SIMON FENCHURCH SERIES

1. THE HOPE THAT KILLS

2. WORTH KILLING FOR
3. WHAT DOESN'T KILL YOU
4. IN FOR THE KILL
5. KILL WITH KINDNESS
6. KILL THE MESSENGER

CORCORAN & PALMER

1. SENSELESS

HELL'S KITCHEN

FRIDAY

20th March 2020

1

KENJO

Can barely sit upright, man. Strapped in tight here, cuffed through the bars in front. Another cough and my throat burns. My chest rattles an' all. Swear it's like that guard is sitting on us again.

The exact same guard prick is standing over us, snide and wide, as my old boy used to say. Snide and wide. Carl Kelleher. Reckons he's a boss in here now, but I think he's just kidding himself. Thinks he's the top boy, though. Big guy, bigger belly, and the most stupid beard thing you'd see outside a gay bar.

Not that I've been in that many, likes.

Most of his beard is hidden behind one of those masks, though, like he's scared of catching this lurgy off yours truly. But that seems to be all they've got to protect them, likes. Thought they'd have those big suits on like in some sci-fi film about a plague, but no. Not even got proper goggles on, man.

Way I planned this, I was expecting a wee bit of privacy, you know? But this fanny isn't leaving us on my Jack Jones any time soon, is he?

His left hand's tucked into his belt, next to his stick. 'Going to be a nightmare disinfecting this after you're out of it.'

I force out another cough, and it's like my old man's death rattle. Christ, I thought this whole corona-wotsit thingmy was supposed to be just like the flu, but maaaaaan.

Hurts like buggery, too, and I know what buggery feels like. People say prison's a better place these days, and in a lot of ways it is, but you try looking this good in HMP Edinburgh and taking a solo shower, then you'll see how quickly some big caveman moseys on over to your stall and forces himself on you. It's not pretty.

Carl The Boss does up the last strap and I can barely move. Chest feels tight as all hell. He's frowning at us. 'You okay there, Kenny?' His voice is like that boy in those *Star Wars* film. The big guy in the black suit, turns out to be the hero kid's father or something. Never watched them as a kid, they were for nerds like, but I've seen them all now. Classics. Lot of time on my hands at Her Majesty's Pleasure.

'Just fine and dandy, knobhead.' The sour expression on his puss makes us laugh. And that's a big mistake, likes. Makes us cough – bang, bang, bang – but nothing comes up. This wee radge virus is giving my lungs absolute laldie and it's not pretty.

'Doesn't sound like you're fine, Kenny.'

I roll my eyes at the big wanker. 'Might need to take us to hospital, eh no?'

He actually laughs. 'Be there soon enough, Kenny.' He looks out the window and frowns again. Got a perpetual one, like he wants people to take him seriously or something, show that he's always thinking about something. But this is deeper, like a normal frown.

Out the smeary windows, the car park is absolutely sodden, soaked like that time I had to lie low near Pitlochry when the filth were after us. Camping's shite at the best of times, but when it's absolutely pelting down for a solid fortnight? Can still taste those beans and sausages, too. Minging.

Anyway, what he's frowning at?

Something squeaks and grinds. Another big fat bastard is pushing another wheelchair towards the van, and the guard boy is waving his hand to get Carl's attention.

So obviously, Carl is *that* kind of arsehole, wants to look like a Secret Service agent protecting President Fucknut in some shitey film, only he's not got the earpiece or the thingamajig in his sleeve, so he has to put his radio up to his bonce. 'Aye, Davie, receiving.'

Can't make out what he's getting from the other screw, but he's not happy about it. Takes a long look at us, then scans around the empty prison van and you can see the cogs whirring in there, trying to conjure up some excuse, but there's no excuse the fanny-mouthed chimp can come up to get out of this.

Carl turns his back to us. If I had a knife, I'd stick it between his ribs. Just to the left a wee touch, slide the blade in until it tickles his heart, then he pops his clogs, just have to free myself and bingo, I'm gone, baby.

But another wave of shivers goes right through us. It's like when you're running from the filth and you have to jump into a river to get away, then you get out and it's like the middle of December and absolutely brass monkeys weather and your three layers of clothes are drenched and the cold just hits you. Your body says, "Cheers, boss, I've got this," and starts shivering. Not teeth-chattering bad, but that whole thing. Absolute nightmare, man.

Carl stares right at us, deep into my eyes, but he's just seeing a sack of coughing meat, not a human being. Whatever I've done in my puff, I deserve some respect and dignity. 'Listen, Davie, I've already got one Covid-19 transfer. Two feels like too much risk, know what I mean? Over.'

Boy's right an' all. Transferring one lag to the hospital, cool beans. Two? Bad news.

Old cellie explained it to me once. Doesn't just double up the problem, but makes it like four times worse. Least, that's how Big Dunc explained it to me. Chaos theory and all that.

Carl's listening hard to the other screw, his forehead creasing that wee bit harder, and eventually he nods. Doesn't say anything, likes. If he is actually a boss now, no matter how much power this fanny thinks he now has, he's still got a boss of his own, and that boss has one too. And there's like this whole global pandemic thing kicking off, load of bats eating people in China and making them cough or whatever.

Still, I'd heard I was getting ghosted. Shoved up to Perth in the middle of the night, cutting me off from my brief just as another appeal comes up. Cutting me off from my old dear, too. Not happening.

But this is happening. Just you watch.

'Fine, then. Over.' Carl stomps across to the back door and sticks his card in the reader, then puts the code in the wee machine. Can't get a good look at it, likes. But timing's everything. Absolutely everything. Big bastard is muttering some shite under his breath, which let's be honest is heavier than the graffiti in a truck stop bogs.

Win-win.

'Okay, son, you can walk the rest.' His buddy steps back. Such a lazy arsehole, standing there with both thumbs tucked into his belt, nodding away like he approves of the operation.

Footsteps thump into the back of the van. Kegsy, and he looks ill. His shaved head is the least of it. Eye bags like golf balls and his skin's all grey.

And sure enough, Davie the guard is huffing and puffing. Big wobbly faced bastard who just stood there while that punk raped us. Makes me feel okay about what's coming to him.

Kegsy sits in front of us and Davie cuffs him in same as me, in front and over the bar. Barely enough slack to breathe and, with what we've got, we need it. And he shoots a wink when the screws aren't looking.

Ho, ho, we're in business.

His cough sounds bad, though. Even worse than mine. Rasping and rattling like he's got mice running around in his lungs.

Carl slaps Davie on the back. 'That's us good to go now, then, before any others start coughing.' Boy huffs out this massive sigh. 'Let's get out of here before they send any more over.' Both screws waddle up to the back and it obviously takes the pair of them to lock the back door.

Still pishing it down out there.

'Right, Kenjo?' Kegsy's voice is thin and I can barely hear it.

The guards have their backs to us now, waddling down to the driver's bit.

Kegsy's pushing back, sticking his scrawny arse up in the air like a dug in heat.

And I know what's coming.

My fingers are acting quick, without thinking. I haul his breeks down and rummage around in nature's boot. Bingo, he's shoved a big lump of plastic up his jacksy.

'Careful.' His voice is a hiss.

I take hold of it, warm plastic all sticky from that bugger's germs, and ease it out. I haul his breeks up again and the van stinks of shite now.

Pair of clowns must spot that something's up here.

Right?

But the engine goes.

So I sit back. Used to be a toothbrush, but it's like a work of art now. I run my thumb across the sharpened end. Nice. Almost cut myself, eh?

The other end, though, has been filed to a handcuff key.

Ho, ho, this is going to be fun.

∽

SOUNDS like the van stops again. Can't see shite, though. I mean, I'm trying to, likes, but this cough, Christ. It hits when I least expect it.

Man, we've been at this for hours. Are we at the hospital yet? Can't bloody see anything out there, just Kegsy in here, and he's looking like he already died. Eyes shut, head listing to the side. Then he coughs, like someone shooting a rifle. Crack, crack, crack. Wakes him up, but he's hardly compos mentis.

Carl and Davie are on their feet now, so that must mean that we're here. Right? They're looking at Kegsy first, mind, probably more worried by that cough of his than my wee tickler. Hope they've got a pan handy cos it sounds like his lungs are coming up any minute.

I ease the shiv round and pop the key into the lock. Bingo, the cuffs pop open. Far too easily, if you ask me. This shiv is the *business*. Kegsy's played a blinder here, though. Who designs these things?

The pair of fannies step out of the driving compartment and walk past.

I sit there like I'm still cuffed in. Now I just have to wait. Still ramming it down out there, but there's no sign of anybody. Car park's completely empty, man.

Carl eases his big fat arse around and wanders over to the door and does the old chip and pin, then slides it to the side. 'You want to start opening the cuffs, Davie?' He steps out into the pissing rain and gets out his moby, then starts talking to someone.

Poor Davie doesn't get a chance to answer.

I'm on my feet and slide the shiv into that sweet spot, unblocked by bone or muscle. Just my blade piercing the prick's heart. Shame to do this to anyone, but then you stand there whistling while some big animal rapes someone in the showers, you're going down. Just regret not getting my rapist, too, but beggars can't be choosers, eh no?

Outside, Carl's making a right royal arse of laying the ramp out, leaving it all higgledy-piggledy.

I sit the boy down on my seat. He's still alive, still hanging on, but he's struggling to speak, struggling for breath. This is the best bit, like, when you watch that light go out behind their eyes. But I've not got time for it today, so I ease off his mask and snap it on myself. Covers everything, doesn't it? Breathing like that big bastard from *Star Wars*. Just need a light saber. Don't want the old dear catching this plague, I tell you. Bad enough on a boy like me or Kegsy.

Davie's boots are nice. Big shiny black things. I pull the tongue down and, oh ho, I'm in luck. Size nines. Quick untie job and my feet are in them. The boots are warm, from a dead man, but you've got to do what you've got to do, eh no?

'DAVIE!' Carl's shout is like a dog barking but like, huffing and puffing through the mask. 'What's stopping you?'

Just the wee matter of dying, Carl.

I head over to the back door and Carl's still fannying about with the ramp.

And he looks up at us.

Bad move. I crack my left boot into his jaw and it's like Leigh Griffiths hammering one in from outside the box.

Take that, you Tory fud!

He rolls off down the ramp, completely out of the game. I take a peek outside and it's still quiet as the prison library, so I grab Carl by the ankles and pull him back up the ramp. I yank off his mask and walk over to Kegsy. 'You okay, bud?'

'I'm dying, mate.' Another cough, so deep it's like it's torn his bowels apart. 'You go without me.'

'Not a chance.' I unlock the cuffs and help him up to standing. 'Here.' I snap the mask over his lugs and pull it over his face.

'Bit late for this, man.'

I'm trying not to laugh here so I don't cough, but I can't help it. Another ten seconds of coughing my guts up. 'It'll be a decent disguise, okay?'

'With you now.'

'You good?'

Kegsy looks at us, like death warmed up. 'Mate, just leave me here.'

'No, no, we're doing this, bud. Come on.' I haul him up to standing and wrap his arm over my shoulder.

And he's okay, actually, now he's upright. Walking on his own steam. 'Cheers, Kenjo. Come on.' He steps over to the door, and the old Kegsy's back, baby!

Now, we just need to find that motor and the keys.

2

BAIN

This hotel room is way too fuckin' small for this. Over this tiny wee table, rammed full of shite, I can smell Elvis's onion-y breakfast. I mean, who eats a fuckin' burrito at this time of day?

Actually there was that one London cop. *'Lunch? Oh, there's a great Mexican down Bumclench Lane.'* Not a bad sort, but he had a real darkness to him.

My phone goes. *Sundance calling...*

I'll be fucked if I'm answering *that*. Takes Cullen a few seconds to leave a voicemail, then he'll be another few to tap out a text and fire it across all those pipes under the Atlantic. At least, that's how Elvis explained it. Could be satellites. Who knows?

I tap my finger off the microphone. 'So, you just about ready here?'

Elvis flicks his nails into my paw. 'I told you to stop touching it.' Those stupid sidies are now almost meeting at his chin after two weeks with yours truly. I mean, he thinks he looks like that boy from the X-Men films, but he's more like that clown from Slade. 'It's not been the same since you dropped it in that swimming pool.'

'That was an accident.'

'Never an accident with you, Bri.'

And here it is, that text from Sundance:

Brian, you need to answer your phone. You're facing an HR investigation. Call me. Scott.

Cheeky bastard. He can ram his HR investigation so hard it comes out his fuckin' mouth.

So I look over at Elvis.

Only, he's holding up his phone. 'Text from Cullen. Says you're to phone him.'

'Aye, that'll be chocolate.' I chuck mine on the bed. 'We going to do this, or what?'

Elvis winces. Not sure what at. 'I'm not sure us still being in New York is the smartest move.'

'Ach, what's the worst that can happen?'

'Well, I can think of a few things.'

Need to count to ten, don't I? 'Paul, let's just record this, have a few beers, then we'll get out to JFK and home. Okay?'

'Fine.' Elvis hits a key on his laptop, then clears his throat a few times. 'Future Elvis, that's us started recording. Cheers, Past Elvis.' Another cough and he puts on that daft smile for recording. Supposed to make your voice sound better, but I'm not a practitioner, shall we say.

'Welcome to another episode of the Crafty Butcher podcast.' Elvis grins at us across the table. 'With me, Elvis...'

'And me, the Billy Boy.' I lean forward, propping myself up on my elbows. Christ I'm tired.

Elvis shuts his eyes as he speaks. 'We're in Hell's Kitchen, New York, recording another episode for our "Jings Across America" series where we've been sampling some of this great nation's best craft beers. We started in Seattle twelve days ago, and have visited Portland, Denver and Austin among many, many highlights. But now for the real highlight, a pub crawl through Brooklyn and Williamsburg, where we'll be enjoying some of New York's best craft beer.'

Elvis is staring at us, for some reason.

So I pick up the baton here. 'And some absolute pish, I fully expect. And this is episode thirteen, which hopefully won't be unlucky for us.' Can just fuckin' picture the reaction when this goes out tonight. The *chortling* over Corn Flakes, or commuters on the bus or in the motor giving themselves a wry smile.

They fuckin' love our patter out here.

I mean, I'm actually grinning. Feels like the first time a job has had this reaction to us in donkey's years.

But that's not why Elvis is staring at me. He shakes his head, the cheeky shite. 'We're recording in our hotel room in Hell's Kitchen. Now, this was supposed to be the preamble to our live show in Williamsburg tonight, but that was sadly cancelled.'

'Aye, cos of this stupid bug going round. Honestly, some people need to get a hold of themselves. It's just the flu.'

Elvis looks like he's shat a house brick. 'Not that we're for one second suggesting that people ignore the official guidelines around safety. Please respect other people's social distance. Two metres minimum.'

'Except it's six feet over here, so they can't even get that right, eh?' I reach over for a perfectly chilled bottle of beer and use that opener with "Dad" stencilled on the metal to prise the cap off. Always breaks my heart when I use it. Should get another one, but the action on this is *sublime*. I take a sip. 'Oh, man, this is like snogging God. Citrusy as cat's piss, but with a real low floor of bitterness. And it's cloudier than a Glasgow morning.'

'What's that you're drinking there, Billy Boy?'

'Just a wee drop of that St Petersberg IPA we got a few bottles of down in Florida. Transferred it up in my dirty laundry bag. Turns out it's not a crime to shift beer over state lines.'

'And luckily only one exploded over your dirty grundies, Billy.'

'Aye, and they smell a lot better now.' A nice little pause to soak up a laugh that I only hear inside my skull. 'Tell you, when we get back to Blighty, they're getting a serious order put in.'

'And from me too.'

'You know we should just gang together to save on shipping it from Florida to Scotland, right?'

'Aye, aye.' Elvis is nodding like I'm stupid. 'When I said—'

'And I know it's eleven in the morning, just on the dot, but

I've got this app on my phone saying where it's five o'clock.' Christ, I have to put my specs on to check. 'But there you go. It's five o'clock in Berlin. Cracking city.'

'And somewhere we'll be visiting in October as part of our "Cans Europe Express".' Every time he says that, Elvis grins like he'd just thought it up. 'Though I suspect we'll be enjoying some bottles and draught beer as well.'

My turn to leave a gap for his applause. 'Speaking of which, Elvis my pal, we've got our special guest appearing live on this show in a few minutes, haven't we?'

'That's right. But before that, here's a word from our sponsors.' He sits back and claps his hands three times. 'Note to Future Elvis: cut out me going "When I said", okay? And think about whether to leave in Brian's crap about Covid being—'

'That's staying in.'

'Fine.' He hits a button on the laptop. 'Okay, that's us for now.'

Another sip of beer and it's that bit less chilled so that bit tastier. 'So where the fuck is he?'

'No idea.' Elvis glances over at the door. 'Still can't believe you've got that bum bag.'

'Fuck sake.' Prick keeps going on about this. 'Call it a fanny pack over here.' I pick it up off the side table. 'I'll have the last laugh when you can't find your travel documents and mine are safely stowed away in this bad boy.'

And bingo, as if by magic, there's a knock at the door.

Elvis paces across the room. 'Christ, why can't you put your dirty pants in a bag like a normal person? Why the hell do you have to leave them all over the floor?' He opens the door and his scowl is replaced by a smile. 'Art?'

'Elvis?'

'Yup.'

And this big fat bastard wraps Elvis up in a bear hug. His massive beard looks like it could house a colony of fuckin' seagulls. And that better be cream cheese and not bird keech encrusted in it. He's got a Bon Jovi-era denim jacket on, complete with patches, and olive green cargo pants. And fuckin' flip-flops. What a total fanny.

But he's over by the table by the time I'm on my feet. 'Art Oscar.' Big massive hand thrust out at us.

'Bri—' I clear my throat, but I'll be fucked if I'm shaking that paw. Christ! 'Just call me Billy.'

'Sure, Bill.' He sits in my fuckin' seat and seems to just melt everywhere. Swear, he's got massive tits and he looks about eight months pregnant. 'It's roasting hot in here. You guys sure like it hot, huh?' He's staring at my bottle. 'Oh, lemme have some of that.' He takes a swig of it and I'll be fucked if I'm touching it again.

What a twat.

I take Elvis's seat and let that sod perch on the edge of his bed. Christ. Have to open another beer, don't I? And those Floridian marvels are all gone now.

'Thought I was gonna be late.' Art gasps as he takes another swig of *my* fuckin' beer. 'But Midtown's like a ghost town today and, I swear, there's no security downstairs so I could just come right up. Crazy, huh?'

'Totes.' Elvis leans forward. 'You good to go?'

Art takes another pull of my beer and starts coughing. Another series of rattles, like a fucking machine gun. Keep expecting him to cough up his kidneys. Christ. 'I'm fine. Hay fever. Tree pollen season right now. Always gets me.'

'Tree pollen?' I don't trust this fanjo one bit. 'Is that a thing?'

'It's birch just now. Wait for maple. Mid-summer, my eyes are streaming and I can't sleep, buddy.'

Elvis raises his eyebrows at the boy. 'You good?'

Art does a big grunting cough and sticks the thumbs up. 'That's me good.'

'Okay.' Elvis reaches round us to hit his laptop keyboard. 'Recording. And three, two, one.' He puts on that presenter smile again. 'And we're now joined by Art Oscar, who was going to be our special guest tonight onstage in Brooklyn, but sadly that's been shelved for now.'

I open another bottle and sink a good bit of it. Decent, but nothing on the one Art fuckin' nicked. 'But we'll be back in the fall, hopefully.'

Elvis gestures at him. 'And Art really needs no introduction.'

Art sips more beer. 'Thanks.'

'But we're going to give you one anyway.' Elvis snatches his bit of paper from in front of us. 'As well as being an award-winning podcaster, he also writes for the *New Yorker* magazine.'

'Used to.' Art slams his beer down on the table. 'I'm now at the *Gothamite*, where I write their craft beer and cocktails column.'

Makes us frown, have to say. 'Cocktails?'

'I swear, you should try the pina coladas in my neighbourhood bar.'

'Take that under advisement, son.'

Boy's frowning at us. 'Sorry?'

'Pina coladas. I mean, come on.'

'Trust me.'

Wish I could. 'So that whole journalism thing's going to shite, then?'

'Why's that?'

'Well, I saw some Instagram posts last night. How you're driving a Travis car, right?'

'Sure. I don't earn enough dough from my writing, so I need to make ends meet somehow. You try living in Manhattan on my salary. But our online stuff is starting to happen.' Art coughs again, then rubs at his throat. 'I do a lot more investigative work too. For instance, there's a piece I'm doing on these anti-5G pills? You hear about them?'

I give the wanker a big scowl, trying to intimidate him. 'Pills for mobile phones?'

'No. These pills stop people... It's hard to explain. The thing in this country, right now, at this moment, is that there's a ton of conspiracy theories going around. Blame whoever you like, social media or the government or Wall Street or the Tea Party or Antifa, whoever, but the world is going cray-cray, man.'

'This disease is part of it?'

'Sure. I mean, call me a tinfoil hat wearer, but I don't see millions of people dying because of it, do you? It's a campaign to overthrow democracy and install a global government.'

Ah shite.

I fuckin' *told* Elvis to vet these nutters before they come on. The good thing is we can just scrub this episode and re-record without this bell end. 'So these gangs are—'

'They're selling these drugs to protect against 5G. I mean, it's pretty obvious it causes this virus, right?'

'Is it?'

And as I'm getting into my fuckin' stride, my fuckin' phone rings again. Golden rule of podcasting is to turn it off before we start, but fuck sake, I needed that prop earlier, didn't I? Berlin…

And ah shite, it's the old boy.

'Pause a sec.' I pick it up and walk over to the window. 'Dad, you okay?'

It's just fuckin' silence, though. The stupid old bugger has butt-dialled again, hasn't he? I knew buying him a mobile was a mistake, but would *she* listen? Would she fuck. So I hang up and text *her*:

Can you check Dad's okay? Just had a call.

I look out the window but it's just another building, brown bricks about two metres away. Social distancing. Christ.

My phone buzzes with a text:

Sure, I'll check when my shift's done. Love you. A x

Attagirl.

Thx.

Back at the table, Elvis is pouring beer into a tall glass for Art. 'So after this, we'll go for some beers, yeah?'

'Sure.' Art sucks down the foam and gasps. Then smacks his lips together. 'Soon as you hit end on that recording, we're getting a Travis across town to Williamsburg. We'll start in a bar near my apartment.'

I take my seat and pick up my own beer. 'You say "a Travis" but I take it you mean your motor?'

'Well, yeah. But it'll get me off the clock.'

'For Billy's sake, that bar better not be the one that sells pina coladas.' Elvis is smiling at me, but I invented that move. Hide a slagging beneath friendliness.

'Sorry about that, boys.' I take my seat again and power off my phone. 'Schoolboy error.'

'I'll edit it out.' Elvis reaches over to the keyboard again. 'So, are we good to go?' But *his* phone rings now. Christ, we look like amateurs here. 'Ah, I better take this.' So he repeats my move and slouches over to the window. 'Dani, hi.'

'I'm a bit puzzled.' Art rubs beer out of his beard, stares at us like I just pissed on his shoes. 'I thought we were going to have a nice friendly chat, but you're interrogating me like you're one of NYPD's finest.'

'Sorry, bud. Might not agree with the powers that be on the severity of this bug, but I've had it up to here with conspiracy nutters.'

'So you're a sheeple, huh?'

Get a load of this fanny. 'Whatever.'

And Elvis barrels over between us. He grabs the TV remote and points it at the big panel on the wall. 'What channel?'

The TV flicks on to the baseball, but it quickly cuts over to some boy in a suit sitting in a fancy studio. Pink shirt, purple tie. Fuckin' knew a boy who wore a get-up like that, but he died.

Label below says Governor Andrew M. Cuomo. Ah shite, this isn't good. 'So we're going to put out an executive order today. Put New York State on pause. Policies that assure uniform safety for everyone. We're all in quarantine now. This is not life as usual. Accept it. Realise it and deal with it.'

The wee ticker at the bottom updates. "New York State Now In Lockdown"

And Elvis glowers at us. '*This* is the worst that can happen.'

3

CULLEN

Acting DI Scott Cullen scurried through the pouring rain as fast as he could. Phone pressed to his ear, ringing and ringing and—

'We're sorry but—'

Voicemail. Again.

He hung up and kept on going.

Mid-afternoon in Portobello and it was miserable. The tide was right in, the foaming sea licking at the defences, the spray loosing off another salvo towards the benches half a mile or so away.

Right where Cullen and his team were headed. Looked like all four of their targets were sitting there, laughing and joking in the miserable weather. What a life.

Sergeant Lauren Reid had to run to catch up with Cullen. Her thin red hair was tied back and soaked, just like her uniform. 'Scott, when you offered me that job, I didn't expect to be back in uniform so soon.' Her southern English accent cut through the howling gale.

'Neither did I.' Cullen chanced a glance down at his own uniform. Time was the T-shirt sleeves would've shown off disco muscles, but time and sloth had withered them. That, and Evie preferring the slimmer look these days. At least his sleeves had pips, despite his position *still* only being Acting.

Who was he kidding? A few years ago, he'd constantly moan to everyone who'd listen about never getting a chance to make sergeant, and now he was on the brink of a full DI position.

Get over yourself, Scott.

Up ahead, their DCs walked lockstep, Craig Hunter alongside Angela Caldwell. Pretty much the exact same height, though Hunter was twice as thick maybe. His ridiculous arms swung loose as they powered along the promenade.

Angela said something and they both laughed, but the wind swallowed whatever it was. Some joke at Cullen's expense, no doubt.

Cullen slowed to a brisk pace now they were nearing. The Dalriada hotel was already shuttered when it should be building up for its busy season. The picnic benches outside were upended and padlocked. 'I'm glad you're here, Lauren. I'm a man short after... Well.'

'That's what you get if you employ numpties.' The word sounded strange in her accent.

'I wish he was just a numpty.' Cullen held up a hand to get Hunter and Angela to slow, catching them just as Hunter turned back to check them. The big sod got the message that Cullen was taking charge, and he stopped, patting Angela's arm to get her to do the same.

Up ahead, the three benches were in a cut-out section of tidal wall. In summer, during normal circumstances, they'd all be filled with families during the daytime, or with teenagers at night, drinking and smoking weed. But today, the first week of restricted movements falling shy of a full lockdown, the benches were taken by Happy Jack and his three wives.

Happy Jack sat on the nearest bench, looking like a turtle. A huge green coat covered over a back hunched by years living on the street, as well as the latest in a long line of rucksacks strapped to his body. Age had softened his ginger hair to a sandy rust, but his bushy beard seemed untainted. His ruddy cheeks were rounded, only squaring off as he took a suck from a bottle of cider. Even with minimum alcohol pricing, Jack could still source ultra-cheap turps to batter his liver with.

Then again, Cullen knew the life Jack had lived. A horrendous childhood, ten years in the army, two of which were in an Iraqi prison, then five in a mental hospital before being let go, only to turn up sporadically, causing mischief. Nothing serious, just scams to help him get by.

And he always had a few wives.

Cullen didn't recognise any of the current lot, but they were like Macbeth's three crones. Ages varying from late teens to thirties to maybe a rough sixties. All dressed in black raincoats, their hoods up against the wind and the rain.

Jack passed his bottle to the nearest one and she took a deep sip. And that was when Jack noticed them. His gaze slipped from the distant view across the Forth – past the island Cullen could never remember the name of – and the rain-soaked hills of Fife beyond, to the cops approaching from two sides. Years of experience kicked in. 'Come on, girls.' Jack jolted upright and set off across the promenade, heading for the back road leading up to the high street.

But Cullen was too quick for him. He left Lauren and jogged over to block their exit. Hunter and Angela obstructed the other path, leaving just the inundated beach behind them.

Nowhere to go.

Jack stopped and stood there, head bowed. He looked over at Hunter and nodded at him. 'You okay, Craig?'

'I'm doing okay, Jack.'

'Been a while.'

'Hasn't it just. How *you* doing?'

'I was fine, Craig. Just fine. But these... You... *Fascist.*'

'Jack.' Cullen gave him a sharp smile. 'No need to be so frosty.'

'Going to lock us up, are you?' The dark side of Happy Jack was out now, his nostrils splayed, teeth bared, eyes narrowed. 'Take us off the streets so it doesn't look so bad for your fascist overlords?'

'No, Jack. We're here with an offer for you.'

That seemed to puzzle him. He gave each of his wives a look, then settled his gaze back on Cullen. 'Go on?'

'I don't know if you've heard how—'

'That virus is a hoax, and we're having nothing to do with it.'

Cullen widened his smile. Exactly how he'd expected this to go. 'Jack, the virus might have everything to do with you.'

'Nonsense.'

'It's true.' Angela made her way around the side to stand next to Cullen, but she was looking at the wives and not Jack. 'We're here to help you. There's a government initiative in place to home people in your situation in a hostel.'

'It's not a *situation*, lassie. This is our *life*.'

'And it could be your death.' Angela let the words settle. 'We need to make sure that all persons of no fixed abode are securely rehomed until this is over.'

'Until what's over? This coronavirus is a myth!'

'No, it's not. It's killing people. Forty-eight people in the UK yesterday. Eight hundred in Italy. Three prison inmates died this week because of it. There's a special ward in Edinburgh Royal Infirmary to cover it. They're opening hospitals in London and Birmingham.' She paused again. 'Now, I know you guys love your freedom, but you're most at risk here. We need to get you off the street, otherwise it's very possible you will die.'

Jack shook his head, just like Cullen had seen a few times in the past.

But it seemed to be getting through to the younger two wives, sharing a worried look. Frowning, twitching eyebrows. Despite their advanced stage of inebriation, they were clearly still capable of processing the information. But they didn't seem brave enough to say anything.

'I know you've not had the best of times, but this is a chance to rebuild your lives. There are courses on offer to help retrain you. And counselling.'

Jack waved a hand at his wives, trying to force them to ignore Angela, then he stared hard at her. 'What do you know about what we've been through?'

Angela looked at the middle of the three wives. 'I know quite a bit about you, Mary.'

Mary's eyes widened. 'What?'

'Mary Armstrong. Abused by your uncle, physically and sexually. One day, he hospitalised you, but still nobody believed you. And then you couldn't face your family, so you took to the streets.'

'How do you know that?'

'I spoke to your old social worker, Ben. He says hi.'

Mary shook her head.

'And Alison McGuire?'

The youngest hung her head low.

'An abusive relationship with a pimp from the age of fourteen. He kept knocking you up and beating you up until you miscarried. So you ran away from Newcastle to Edinburgh.'

The oldest one didn't want to look at her, didn't want her own demons aired. 'I'll take a room.'

Cullen smiled at her. 'Thank you, Elaine. I think you'll enjoy it there.' He looked at the other two. 'What about you?'

He got a nod from them both.

Jack sighed. 'You're not taking no for an answer, are you?'

'Correct.'

A meat wagon trundled along the back road towards them, pulling up just behind Cullen.

'So, what's it to be, Jack?'

'Fine. But I want your word that we can get back to our lives once this is all over.'

'It's what everyone wants, Jack. Just take care of yourself in there, okay?'

'Sure thing.'

'Craig, Lauren, can you escort them?'

And they did, smiling through the downpour as they led them up to the waiting meat wagon.

Angela walked over to Cullen. 'At least they don't have much stuff to gather up. My fingers are still sticky from Loose Morag's shopping trolley.'

'Good work there.' Cullen grinned at her. 'Persuading them to come in like that. If that'd just been me and Craig, they'd have run and we'd be hunting them until dusk.'

She shrugged it off. 'Just doing my job.'

'No, you're not *just* doing anything. You're doing a sergeant's job, and doing it really well. Going above and beyond. Don't see Craig or Elvis calling up social workers to discuss age-old cases.'

She might've been blushing slightly. 'Thanks, Scott.'

Cullen's phone rang. He checked the display. Yvonne Flockhart. Still her Sunday name, not his favourite short form. 'Better take this.'

Angela nodded at him, but didn't look in his direction. 'Cheers.' She followed Hunter and Lauren over to the van.

'Evie…'

'Hey, Scott.' She gave one of those deep yawns that didn't seem to want to let go of its host. 'Sorry.'

'You sound knackered.'

'Yup. Just calling to say we've caught a bad one. Probably won't be home until later, so I won't be able to meet up tonight.'

'Right.' And it hit Cullen hard. An hour left on his shift, spent dealing with all sorts of malarkey, and the thing he'd been clinging to was seeing Evie later.

Shit, their relationship *was* serious.

He cleared his throat. 'I've heard they're talking of extending the restrictions to a full lockdown.'

'Really?'

'Just what I heard.' It sounded brittle even to him. 'Means we won't be able to see each other.' He left a pause. 'I'll miss you.'

Sounded like she smiled. 'I know. I'll miss you too.'

'Sure I can't tempt you down to Leith whenever you finish tonight?'

'It's a loooong drive from Livvy, Scott, and you know it.'

'I'll make it worth your while. Got an organic chicken in the fridge and—'

'You had me at "make it worth your while", but if you make some of that chilli gravy?'

'See what I can do.'

And his police radio chose right then to crackle into life. 'Control to DI Cullen.'

He sighed. 'Better take this. Let me know what's happening, Evie.'

'Will do.' She paused. 'I like you, Scott.'

'Like you too.' He hung up, but he knew that stupid joke would hurt one or both of them. Unless it progressed from like to love.

He put the radio to his ear. 'Receiving, over.'

'Got a call in, Scott. Someone's burning a 5G mast in Piershill.'

∼

CULLEN PUSHED his foot to the floor and weaved the pool car around a long queue of traffic. Felt like the last days of Christmas shopping here. Weren't people supposed to be staying at home? He pulled back in and hit a wall of black smoke pouring across the road. No idea where it was coming from.

Up ahead, Hunter's squad car cut across traffic into the Ashworth's car park.

Cullen followed him in. The supermarket car park was rammed full. He had to slam the brakes to stop him from hitting a man pushing a trolley full of packed meat. He had half a mind to have a word with the guy and check that it was all for him. Knowing his luck, it'd be for a homeless shelter.

Cullen pulled up at the edge next to Hunter's car and got out. He immediately caught sight of the reason for their call out.

Next door to the supermarket was a row of shops, the kind you'd see in any Scottish suburb. A squat post-war building housing a bookies, a pub and a fast-food takeaway, with pizza and kebabs by the look of it. Most locals would hit them in that order too.

On top was a shiny new phone mast, looking barely days old, but smouldering with the black smoke of a petrol fire. A pair of masked men were up there, holding out a bed sheet that read "5G = DEATH".

'They're not all locked up, are they?' Hunter joined Cullen by his car. 'This not part of that 5G squad's remit?'

'Yup.' Cullen unfastened his baton and set off towards the

pub's back door. 'On their way over from Torphichen Street.' He knocked on the door and waited. 'Methven put his hand up and offered our help.'

'There's nothing he won't do to get us work, is there?'

'That's the problem with only being Acting, Craig.'

'Right.' Hunter tried the door and it opened. 'Sod this.' He stepped inside.

No signs of life in there. No music, no horse racing on the TV, no drinkers starting a half-three singalong. But, behind a door, there was a set of steps up to the roof.

'Must be how those dafties got up there.' Hunter led on up, taking it slowly, his own baton extended.

Cullen followed him out into the howling rain. Only a floor up, but it felt like they were on an oil platform. And it stank of smoke. Dank, rancid smoke. He put his finger to his lips and, baton raised, approached the masked idiots. 'Police!'

They dropped their bed sheet and turned round. Both big guys, but fat and hopefully not a match for Cullen and Hunter. Then again, Cullen had seen the counter-proof to the saying: the bigger they were, the harder they'd crush the air out of your lungs when they landed on you.

The nearest one produced a knife, glinting in the soft daylight.

'Here we go again...' Cullen stepped closer and raised his baton even higher. 'Sir, I need you to come with us.'

'Fuck you, pig!'

The faintest wail of a siren. Fire brigade. Perfect. Bunch of wankers would keep winding Cullen and Hunter up for years if they didn't take these plonkers down and soon.

So Cullen lashed out and cracked his baton off the knife-wielder's forearm. The knife tinkled to the ground and Cullen raced forward, kicking it clean away towards the stairs. He grabbed the guy's arm and bent it behind his back, then pushed him face down onto the bitumen. He was struggling to breathe from all the smoke. 'Name and address.'

'Fuck you, pig!'

Someone screamed.

Cullen looked over.

Hunter was wrestling the other guy to the ground. He had a PPE mask on, but it slipped up.

And shite, Cullen recognised him. Keith Ross. Worked in the Ashworth's between Gilmerton and Liberton. A cleaner, if he remembered right. 'Get off me!'

'Go on, Craig, let him up. Then arrest him.'

So Hunter did, slackening his grip on his arms and letting the big guy up. 'Keith Ross, I'm arresting you for the—'

Keith spat, a lumpy volley of gob flying through the air and landing in Hunter's mouth just before he could shut it. 'COVID!'

4

BAIN

For fuck's sake.

I can't take my eyes off the telly. It's switched to some boys back in the studio, all talking shite, but I can't hear what they're saying from all the noise in my head.

That governor boy is keeping us here, isn't he? We're trapped in this fuckin' city.

Feels like a bit of an overreaction to say the least. A few people getting a cough and they shut the whole world down? Try doing that in Glasgow. They'll be on the fuckin' streets. Have to bring in the army!

Art gets up and slopes off to the bog, coughing into his fist.

'Okay, Dani. I'll let you know.' Elvis sits on the edge of the bed, fizzing.

He stares right at us, shaking his head. 'She's not happy.'

'Don't doubt it.' I can barely bring myself to look at him, though. He's blaming me, isn't he? And he's right to.

'Paul, I'm sorry. This is my fault.'

'Damn right it's your fault. We should've gone home from Orlando, or even back in Austin. "Connecting flights, though, Elvis, they'll be a nightmare at Heathrow, eh?" So you argued and you won. And we're stuck in New York. This is a complete disaster.'

'Okay, you can kick my balls when we're out of this. Right now, I suggest we think about what we're going to do about it.'

'What *we're* going to do? This is on you, Brian.' Never seen Elvis like this. He's fuckin' seething. 'You told me this would be fine. What's the worst that could happen, eh? Well, being stuck in New York while your pregnant wife is helpless at home is pretty much the definition.'

'I'll call the airline, see about getting us on the next plane.'

'And if that doesn't work?'

'Then we've still got our flights tomorrow.'

'You honestly think they won't be grounded?'

He's got us there. I've no idea, either way. I mean, if you have a sniff, then nae danger you're getting on a flight. 'The Home Office will sort us out.'

'Aye, but when? Dani's in her eighth month, Brian. Push is coming to shove.' He winces. 'Pardon the pun.'

'Look, if it all goes to shite, it'll only be for a few days. We can get pissed and see it out here in NYC. Chance to see the city.'

'I'm not staying here!'

This is all my fault. Getting carried away with Jings Over America. Ignoring everything. 'I'm really sorry, Paul.'

'I know what this is all about. I shouldn't have told you that you're going to get screwed by Cullen and Methven back in Edinburgh. Shouldn't have listened to you that this will be our big break.'

'Sorry.'

'You keep saying that, but I wish you'd actually mean it. Just once.'

I get out my mobile. 'Right, I'm calling the airline, okay?'

I OPEN the room door and it's stinking of farts in there. Holding a tray of the last three coffees in New York and a box of shite doughnuts. Fuck sake.

Elvis and Art are sitting at the table. Not even drinking. Elvis looks over at me. 'Well?'

'Got some coffees in while I was on hold.'

'I meant, did you get through to them?'

How do I break this to him? With a joke? 'Bastards aren't flying without a negative test.'

'Seriously?'

'No, I'm winding you up.' I plonk the coffees on the table. 'Here. Couldn't get on any today without going via fuckin' Australia, but our flight's still scheduled for tomorrow.'

Art opens the lid on his and frowns, then his face lights up like a wee laddie. 'What time you guys flying?'

'Eight a.m. flight to Heathrow, then six hours waiting there, then a flight to Edinburgh.'

'They don't fly direct?'

Yet another bone of contention.

Elvis takes a sip of coffee. 'That's damn fine coffee.' He puts the lid back on. 'They *do* fly direct, but *someone* doesn't like the airline, do they?'

Pricks are both looking at me. 'I've got a shit ton of points with—'

'Guys, how about you get loaded with me tonight.' Art finishes his coffee and crumples up the carton. 'I could get a buddy over with a buttload of beer in ten minutes. Like Phil Collins sang, just say the word.'

I stare at him like this is a laughing matter. 'Phil fuckin' Collins?'

'Hey, don't diss him.' Art's got his moby out. 'Bottles, cans, even a minikeg. And I'll make sure you guys are on that jet tomorrow.'

He's speaking my language. 'Sure?'

'Sure. Trust me.' He opens the box of doughnuts. 'Hoo boy. Are these vegan?'

'As vegan as the milk in your coffee.'

'That was a black coffee.'

Shite. He's drunk mine. I open the lid and there's a load of foam. Oat milk foam. And I fuckin' hate lattes. Twat. 'Aye, they're vegan.' Whatever. 'Okay, get those beers here.'

'Sweet.' He gets out his phone and starts stabbing the screen with a trotter.

'Need to phone the little lady.' I take my coffee back out into the hallway.

For once, it doesn't sound like we're living in a squat, with thumping and shouting bleeding through the walls. Just merciful peace and quiet.

I hit dial and take a drink of foamy coffee.

'Brian.' It's noisy where she is.

'You okay, love?'

'I'm at work and it's really bloody busy.'

'Okay, okay. It's just that New York's in lockdown.'

'You say that like I should be surprised. You knew this was coming, didn't you?'

Fuck it, better play along here. 'Of course I did. It's just… When it happens, it's a kick in the balls. I mean, I spoke to the airline and our flight tomorrow should be good. But…'

'You didn't try and get an earlier one?'

'Fully booked.'

'Look, it's tough that you're not here, but you're a big boy. You'll cope. This will be one to tell the grandkids.'

'Very true.' I take a slurp of coffee and it's actually bloody lovely. Like they dingied us on the oat milk and stuck real milk in. 'So how's work?'

'Bloody busy, like I just told you. I've got to go. Love you.'

'Love you too.' The line's dead, but my heart isn't. Can't believe it took forty-five years to find my soulmate, but there she is.

I finish the coffee and dump it in the recycling bin.

Okay, the way to play this is to take charge, show those pricks who's boss.

And get absolutely fuckin' banjaxed.

I stretch out and give myself a shake, pump the old lymphatic system, then swipe back into the room. 'When's this mate of yours supposed to turn up, then?'

Art's staring at his phone. 'Not far off. And you can trust me on that beer. Lemon stouts and raspberry sours all the way, baby.'

'Fuckin' hell.' That's like drinking *lager* these days. 'Okay, so how about we tuck in to our bottles first?'

There's a shitload of them and it'll be fuckin' hard trying to get them back to the UK at the best of times. Bastards!

'I'm worried that we're going to miss our flight tomorrow.' Elvis has a sour look on his face, like he's drinking one of Art's hipster beers. 'Our plane's early, like eight. And we need to be there four hours before that, right? And you know what happens when you get a taste for it, Bri.'

Art's scowling, but his eyes are locked on the beer. 'Who's Bri?'

'I mean Billy. You know what I'm saying, Billy?'

'Promise you, Elvis, we'll get that flight tomorrow.'

'Our check-in's like eighteen hours away or something.'

'So if we finish up here at seven, then get some kip, head over at three in the morning, we'll have plenty of time.'

He doesn't look happy.

But he's quiet, at least.

So I get out the placcy bag and pass over some chilled Gundog IPA. 'Here.'

Art's hungry fingers are inspecting the bottle, aren't they? Filthy bastard.

'Here.' I hand him the bottle opener.

He uses it to twist the caps off the three bottles. 'Oh, that is one sweet-ass action.'

'You can keep it.'

He's frowning at us. 'It says "Dad" on it?'

'My son's dead to me.'

'You wanna talk about it?'

'Do I fuck.'

'O-kay.' Art sips the drink. 'Now that is a mighty fine beer, even if I did brew it myself.'

'What?'

'Well, I work *with* Gundog. Help them perfect it, shall we say. Told them to put citra hops in and—' He blinks hard. Then again. The fuck? He rubs at his chest, left side too.

I put my beer back down, un-drunk. 'You okay, bud?'

'My chest's—' He rubs at his wattle neck. 'Some difficulty breathing. Been going on for a week.'

'Sounds like more than hay fever, bud. And it's too early in the year for it to hit that bad. You should be in hospital.'

'Hospital? That's where all the sick people are.' Art's still rubbing his chest. 'I just gotta drain the lizard.' He gets up, but he's coughing really badly now, gasping for fuckin' air. And he's pressing his chest like he's fuckin' dying. And grimacing.

'Elvis, he's having a fuckin' heart attack!'

5

CULLEN

Cullen sipped from his coffee cup as he walked along the corridor. Bitter and harsh, but it fitted his mood to a T. He turned the corner and almost bumped into Lauren. 'Watch it!'

'Oh, sorry.' She was still staring at her phone. 'See they've announced a lockdown in New York?'

Cullen shut his eyes and let out a deep sigh. He knew something like that would happen, tried to warn *you know who* but would the daft sod listen? He reopened his eyes and took another sip of coffee, though it tasted slightly sweeter. 'Where's Happy Jack?'

'Our friend and his wives are in that hotel on...' She clicked her fingers a few times. 'What's the street up from Portobello? Near the park?'

'By the new school?'

'Yes.'

'Duddingston Park?'

'That. There's a chain hotel that's being repurposed as a homeless shelter.'

Cullen finished his coffee and tossed the empty in the recycling. 'Good to hear.'

'Angela's still up there with them.' Lauren wrapped her

arms around her torso. She seemed to be in a constant state of shivering. 'She's good, isn't she?'

'The best.' Cullen couldn't help but smile. 'Worked with her since she was in uniform. Hated it when she quit, but it's great having her back.'

'Thanks for letting me have her on my team. How's Craig?'

'Up at the infirmary.'

'Ouch.' She grimaced. 'Can't believe that sick bugger *spat* in his mouth.'

'I know.' Still made Cullen's gut lurch. 'Hard to imagine much worse.'

'We okay to interview him if he has got Covid-19?'

'Methven cleared it. Need to book a deep clean afterwards, mind.'

'Well, just as well I got these.' Lauren reached into a bag and held up a mask. 'Not the full N95 shebang, but it'll help shield us from the worst of it.'

'Great.' Cullen took his and tried to fit it on. But he couldn't get it to attach to his ears quite right. 'Buggering thing.'

Lauren already had hers on. 'You look the type of man who doesn't like wearing a condom.' At least that's what he thought she said.

Cullen decided to let it pass. Didn't want her to know about his abject fear of getting anyone pregnant. 'Never thought we'd be interviewing people like we were attending a crime scene.'

She reached over and got it to tuck behind his left ear. 'You ready?'

'Sure.' Cullen opened the door for her.

Inside, Keith Ross sat on his own, head bowed and gripping his knees like he was on a particularly turbulent flight.

'Actually, can you get it rolling? I need to make a call.' Cullen stepped away and by the time she was in and recording, the door had slid shut.

And the call was answered. 'Forensic Investigations.'

'Hey, it's Scott.'

Charlie Kidd sighed down the line. Never one to hide his feelings, but this was naked hostility. 'I'm not done with it.'

'But you are doing it?'

'For what it's worth, aye.'
'And?'
'And what?'
Cullen shot back with a sigh of his own. 'Are you getting anything from it?'
'Just so we're clear, what's the "it" I'm supposed to be getting something from?'
'That little USB drive we found in his pocket.'
'Right.' Some loud clicking in the background. 'Not sure what there is to get. I'm just opening it and there's... nothing.'
'Nothing?'
'Aye. It's like there's not even nothing too. It's not registering.'
'Like I expected. Okay, can you bring it down to...' Cullen checked the door, '...room three?'
'Now?'
'No, next Tuesday at half past three.' Another sigh. 'Of course I mean now.'
'Right. Ten minutes.'
Before Cullen could complain, Charlie was gone. But they had more than enough to be getting on with in the meantime, so Cullen opened the door and walked in, staring hard at Keith Ross.
The big guy wasn't looking at anything other than his size thirteens. Cullen wasn't even sure he had his eyes open. Unmasked, he was sporting a chunky beard, not far off the length needed for entry to the average craft beer tap room on Lothian Road. The slogan on his T-shirt was distorted by his man boobs, but looked like it read "COVID-5G".
'Afternoon, Keith.' Still didn't make eye contact. 'Nice T-shirt.'
That worked. Keith looked up, and his pupils were like saucers. Guy was *baked*. Cullen couldn't smell anything from him, but Keith looked a few bong loads into a major stoner session. Bit of a surprise that he'd set fire to the mast instead of himself. But he still didn't say anything.
'I see you've descended even further down the conspiracy rabbit hole since our last meeting.'

Keith frowned. 'Do I know you?'

'You're the cleaner at the Ashworth's in—'

'Oh, I remember you now. Christ. Where's the wee fanny with the shaved head?'

'He's not here. But DS Reid and myself are.' Cullen scraped back the chair and perched on it. 'So. You want to tell us what you were up to on that roof?'

'Nope.'

'That whole "it may harm your defence if you do not mention when questioned something which you later rely on in court" thing, right?'

'Pretty much. I know my rights.'

'Hope you've got a good lawyer.'

'Don't need one.'

'Sure about that?'

'They're all shysters in cahoots with the deep state.'

So anti-Zionism was entering the mix, if not outright antisemitism. 'Lawyers always tell their clients to say "no comment". Know why?'

Keith looked like he barely understood the words were English, let alone had an answer. 'Why?'

'Because then you can pay them to represent you at a trial. It's like a car salesman telling you not to change your oil, means you buy more cars. Ideally from them.'

'This is bollocks, man.'

'What's your message? What do you want to be known for? Burning a telephone mast? What's your message for *Reporting Scotland* at half six tonight?'

'It's...' Keith stared up at the ceiling and his Adam's apple poked through the flab and stubble on his neck. He looked down at Cullen and it was like seeing a drunk sober up in seconds. Fire burnt in his eyes. 'You know what those things are for?'

'Enlighten me.'

'This whole pandemic, it's a tactic from the New World Order. This is them executing their plan to take over and install a World Government.'

'That so?'

'Don't expect you to believe me.'

'So how was burning a phone mast stopp—'

'Those masts are transmitting Covid-19.'

'How?'

'It's all on Google, just search for it.'

'But sure if it's a virus, that's a biological entity that's transmitted between people by various means. How does a mobile phone mast make that happen?'

'It's not a virus. That's a myth. This fictional disease has the exact same symptoms as radiation poisoning.'

Cullen nodded for a few seconds. 'You were very brave, then.'

'Uh, why?'

'Well, you and your mate went up on to that rooftop and got *really* close to the mast. Close enough to set fire to it. Must've put you in harm's way.'

'Thanks, man. Just trying to save others, eh?'

Part of Cullen wished it wasn't this easy. But most of him was glad. 'So you're doing this because...?'

'The NWO are killing people they don't want. Okay? See who this...' he did bunny ears '...this "virus" kills? Old people. People with underlying health conditions. People of BAME origin.'

'Okay, so why don't they target truth-tellers like you?'

'Well, they do.' Keith smirked. 'That's what's going on here.' He ran his finger between Cullen and Lauren. 'You're working for the man, trying to stop me. Aren't you?'

'Keith, we're stopping you harming essential infrastructure.'

'That mast is a biological weapon.'

'No, Keith. It's not even a 5G mast. Not the sort you're talking about. Millimetre wave, right? Gigabit download speeds? Right?'

Keith stared at Cullen like he was Moses and he was getting an audience with Yahweh.

'That flavour of 5G is the tech that'll change a lot of things, but the nearest mast is on Bishopsgate in London. The 5G you're targeting here is just an upgrade to 4G. Faster, but the same underlying technology.'

Keith's mouth was still hanging open. Daft sod believed everything he heard, but didn't check to see if any of it was true. 'Where did you get that from?'

'A friend who works in the sector. He'll be along soon to answer any questions.'

'Right.' But Keith's gaze was back up at the ceiling. Cullen had lost him again.

Time to move on. 'How are those pills working for you?'

'What pills?'

Cullen reached out and – bang on cue – Lauren handed him the first evidence bag. 'Your pockets were full of these tablets.'

'I want them back.'

'So they are yours?' Cullen inspected the blister pack closely. Looked professionally done. 'So these "Anti-5G Pills" are supposed to "Protect you & your loved ones from the Jew World Orders PLAN".' He shook his head. '*Jew* World Order. Really?'

'You want to look up the boy who—'

'What's in them?'

Keith shrugged. 'Protects against 5G.'

'Not Covid-19?'

'Same thing.'

'So what's in them?'

'Don't know.'

'See, there are some on sale that contain chloroquine diphosphate.'

'Sounds right.'

'You know what chloroquine diphosphate is used for?'

'Anti-malaria, but it works against 5G.'

'How long you been selling them?'

'Not long. Just got hold of them on Monday.'

'So you are selling them?'

'Correct.'

'You going to tell me who to, or do I have to go through your texts, calls and emails?'

Keith sniffed. Someone like him would have everything hidden behind a ton of encryption. But people like Charlie

Kidd were getting better and better at outfoxing it. 'Sold a ton to some boy out in Livingston. Few clients in Edinburgh too.'

'Need names.'

'Nope.'

'Your mate will tell us, I suspect.'

Keith grinned. 'You don't even know *his* name, do you?'

Cullen felt a burning sensation up the back of his neck. 'You know that to allegedly protect against Covid-19, you should be selling hydroxychloroquine sulfate.' He shook the evidence bag. 'These are for clearing out fish tanks. Kills the parasites living on some species. Trouble is, it has a tendency to kill people too.'

Keith's mouth hung open. 'What?'

'People will die because of these pills.'

Keith was shaking his head. 'Bullshit.'

'You are a much bigger risk to public health and safety than any perceived threats, you stupid bastard.' Cullen gave him a few seconds. 'I thought your employer would be pretty busy just now, what with people panic-buying. Thought they'd need a cleaner.'

'Place is full of sheep, man. Following the herd.'

'Hell of a lot of cleaning going on just now, I imagine.'

'Telling me, man.'

'So why aren't you at work?'

'I'm self-isolating.'

'So you *have* got Covid-19?'

'Right.'

'You've been tested?'

Keith frowned. 'No. Erm, boss got me to call the doctor, right? Spoke to the boy, and he told me to stay at home. Know exactly how I caught it.'

Lauren rolled her eyes at Cullen. 'No doubt there's a 5G mast by the store?'

'Hardly. Caught it from a customer.' Keith dragged his gaze from the ceiling tiles to look at Cullen. 'Remember the boy. Regular, old guy, came in and was checking out the reduced items, but he was coughing his lungs up, man. And I was supposed to clear away the produce, stick it in the bin. After what happened there last month, the boss is keen to get stuff cleared off quick smart.' He sighed. 'So I took these packets of mince, and they were like brown, but this boy wasn't letting go. And he starts coughing really badly and I told him to get away but he wouldn't. Five days later I'm coughing and burning up.'

Lauren flashed up her eyebrows. 'Sounds like you've got it, alright.'

'Must have, eh?'

Cullen had a slight amount of sympathy for him. An essential worker in a supermarket, subjected to *that* behaviour, then contracting it?

And Keith Ross's mental health wasn't the best to start with, hence a further plunge down the rabbit hole. Self-isolating in front of YouTube videos and the constant push towards more and more extreme content. And someone like him would know where else to access that material, the stuff *they* don't want you to see and *PLEASE* buy my vitamin pills.

But still, he was way out of line. 'So that's why you decided to spit in DC Hunter's mouth?'

Keith sat back, arms folded. 'No comment, eh?'

'While DC Hunter is pretty fit and healthy, his girlfriend is of BAME origin.'

'Which is she? Black, Asian, Middle Eastern?'

'Asian. Her family's from Pakistan. Having to separate is going to be tough on them.'

'I'd apologise, but he's a tool of the state, man. You all are.'

The door opened and Charlie Kidd stepped in, his long ponytail dangling almost in sync with the evidence bag. 'Finished that test, Scott.'

Cullen walked over to the door and took the bag from him with a wink that Keith couldn't see. 'So?'

'Well, it's as we expected.' He leaned in to whisper, 'It's ready.'

'I want that back.'

Cullen turned round to face Keith but inspected the bag. Inside was a USB pen drive, the kind you'd store documents on. 'Why? You pay a lot for it?'

'Four hundred bar. And it's important, man.'

Cullen raised his eyebrows. 'What's it supposed to do?'

'It's...' And Keith looked sheepish now, running his hand over his mouth. 'It's a wearable holographic nano-layer catalyser.'

'And what's one of them?'

'We were going to stick it on that mast to balance out the electric fog that causes the bug.'

'So what happened?'

'Well, we couldn't find a USB port, so we just torched it.'

'Huh.' Through the bag, Cullen pulled the small device apart with a satisfying snap.

'You've broken it!'

Cullen tossed the bag onto the table. 'There's nothing to break.'

'That was four hundred quid!'

'Keith, it's just an empty box with a light on it. There's no nano-layer catalyser. No nothing. And you paid four hundred quid for it.'

Keith was scratching his neck. 'Shite.'

'What's up?'

'It's not just the one. I've got a hundred of them. Took out a loan to pay for it.'

Cullen wanted to laugh, but he wanted to stop this nonsense right here, right now. 'Okay, so the people who sold you this, do you see how they're exploiting you?'

Keith was nodding.

'Right now, we can drop the charges for you doing what you did to that mast, but I'm going to need the name of your mate next door, and the ringleaders of the local anti-5G conspiracy group you're in.'

'But we're fighting for freedom, man.'

'No, you're fighting for your own freedom here. I want a full confession.'

And he had him. Keith just sat there, head bowed. 'Fine. I made the pills myself. Got hold of a big batch of fish tank cleaners, and I repackaged them.'

'And you've been selling them?'

'Just trying to help people, man!'

'And you're killing them.'

'No, man.'

'It might be unknowingly, but you're still responsible. Now, I need the names of your collaborators.'

'It's just me, man.'

'Names. Now.'

Keith stared back up at the ceiling. 'Seriously, it's just me. I don't trust many people.' He looked back down at Cullen. 'You got a bit of paper for me to sign, or what?'

THE OBSERVATION SUITE was like a sauna, hot and sweaty. And it stank like stale running shoes.

DCI Colin "Crystal" Methven sat in front of the giant stack of monitors, arms folded, expression unreadable. He stood up and paced around the room like he was running another triathlon, though his wild eyebrows looked like they were competing in some other sport, one where lots of wide, tall players pack into a small space on the pitch. Rugby, maybe. He settled on the edge of the desk and refolded his arms. And beamed like the proud dad whose kid had just got into Oxford. Or something. 'Excellent work, you two.'

Cullen struggled to make eye contact with him. In a lot of ways he'd much rather face a punch in the balls than a *compliment*. 'Thank you, sir.'

'I mean it. The way you destroyed his logic in there.' Methven settled his gaze on Lauren. 'I know this is a bit of a baptism of fire for you, Sergeant, but you're learning from one of the best here.'

She nodded at him. 'I'm enjoying working with Scott, sir.'

Methven scowled at her. 'I didn't mean him.'

'Oh.'

Methven grinned. 'Of course I meant him.' He leaned over to pat Cullen's arm. 'One of the very best.'

Cullen was glad he was still wearing the protective face-mask. 'So, we'll just cha—'

'No, Scott. The 5G taskforce are on their way here to process

Mr Ross and his friend.' Methven frowned. 'I didn't realise people were called Archie these days. But anyway, excellent work from the both of you.'

'And Charlie Kidd, sir.'

'Well, indeed. A veritable masterstroke. Will he get much out of the batch of devices, do you think?'

'There's nothing inside them, and that one was clean of prints, so I wouldn't hold out much hope.'

'Well.' Methven walked over to Lauren, standing right in her personal space. 'Unfortunately, I've been asked to second you to that operation.'

Lauren glared at him like she was going to punch his lights out. But instead she just stood there, shivering. 'I've only just got here, sir.'

'Well, Inspector Buchan was adamant he needed you.'

Lauren slumped into a seat, shaking her head.

Cullen had no idea what had been going on between them, but it looked serious. 'Sir, can we have a chat?' He opened the door and stepped out into the corridor, then waited for the door to shut. 'Is there anything I can—'

'Sorry, Scott, but that's the deal. Straight from the top.'

'You know that with DS Bain going off the reservation to New York, I haven't got a sergeant, right?'

'New York.' Methven shook his head. 'I saw the news. Stupid sod shouldn't be there. Have you—'

'I'm the last person he'll call. He's still bouncing mine too.'

'There are sodding idiots out there burning phone masts while the world dies. I don't know if you've noticed, but we're not exactly inundated with murder inquiries. I appreciate you want to be out there working on sexy murders, but sometimes we have to do the numpty patrol. We can't just keep people here because of our egos. In times of crisis, we need to help out other departments.'

Cullen knew he was right, but it didn't make it feel any less like he was being kicked in the teeth. 'How about I get an Acting DS?'

'Well, neither Craig Hunter nor—'

'Not Craig. Besides, I think he'll be off the board for a while.'

'Is Simon Buxton back?'

'He's still off sick, sir. Those teeth aren't exactly growing back.'

Methven's eyes gleamed. 'Paula?'

'Not sure she's ready, sir. I was thinking of DC Caldwell.'

Methven frowned for a second. Then his phone blasted out in his pocket. He glanced at his smartwatch. 'Better take this.' He tapped the watch and spoke into it like he was Dick Tracy.

'Colin, I've got a case for you.' Cullen recognised the voice coming out of the watch. DCS Carolyn Soutar, her snooty tone like someone was scraping a blackboard with a smashed bottle. 'There was an incident involving a prison van transporting prisoners from HMP Edinburgh to ERI's specialist Covid-19 ward. Two have escaped. One of the guards has been stabbed.'

'On it.' Methven grabbed his coat and got up. 'Well, Scott. There's your sexy murder.'

6

BAIN

'Help him!' I'm on my feet now, storming across the hotel room, firing into action. And clattering my knee into the table. 'Fuckin' hell!' Bastard thing digs right into my thigh but – *Christ* – that boy's dying here and he needs a hand.

Of course, my medicine bag is right at the fuckin' bottom of my case, isn't it? And there we go, the wee bottle of aspirins. I try to pop one out, but my hand's shaking like a bastard.

Take it slow!

And there we go, a wee white pill right in my paw. So I walk back over to the boy.

But he's looking *fucked*. Barely breathing, holding his chest tight.

And Elvis doesn't look that much better. Just staring at him, like that'll help anybody.

'Paul! Call 911!'

'Right, right.' For once, the stupid wankspanner doesn't know how to hold his phone the right way up. 'Right.'

I hold the aspirin out to Art. 'Right pal, chew on this.'

Elvis has his moby against his ear. 'Shite, there's a queue.'

'For 911?'

'Right.' Elvis shakes his head. 'This is...'

'Elvis, we have to help this boy.' I pour out some water from my night bottle and help Art swallow the pill down, but he's struggling with it. Water spills down his front. 'We've got to take him to hospital! Call them!'

'What do you think I'm doing here?'

Fuck sake. No use arguing, so I get out my phone and tap in 911, then hit dial.

'9-1-1, what is the location of your emergency?'

Elvis gets a glare and a half. Useless prick. 'Hi, a boy's having a heart attack and—'

'Sir, I'm having trouble understanding your accent.'

Fuckin' hell.

Take a deep breath, put on your best police officer voice. 'Sorry, ma'am, is this any—'

'Still struggling to hear you, sir. Are you Irish?'

Irish?

Don't give me that shite.

Only one option here. An old trick that worked on a sojourn down there a few years back, where I had to give them a blast of rubadub Cockney. And not even good Cockney, either, the kind of Hollywood Mary Poppins bollocks that'd get you lynched in Lambeth or Bow, but I tell you. Had them creasing themselves. Not that this is a laughing matter.

So she gets the finest John Wayne off of us. 'Yeah, sure, ma'am, so this fella's having a heart attack.'

'Okay, that's a lot better. You're in the old Note Hotel in Hell's Kitchen?'

Wonder of wonders how they can figure that out. 'Sure am, ma'am.'

'Sir, I'm afraid all emergency responders are presently occupied.'

'You're kidding me.'

'Sir, we're the epicentre of a global pandemic. In normal circumstances, it could be normal to wait half an hour. On a day like this, I can't offer anything.'

Absolutely fucked here. 'Look, how about we get him to you? Where's your nearest hospital?'

'Uh, that'll be Mount Sinai West, eight blocks from you.'

'Thank you, ma'am.' And I hang up. Fuck sake. I look up

the place on my phone and I didn't think that's how you spelled Sinai, but there you go.

Elvis is rubbing a hand down the boy's back, but it doesn't look like it's doing much to help his plight. 'He's not going to be able to walk there, Bri.'

'No, but his motor's downstairs.'

∼

FEELS LIKE I'M IN A FUCKIN' crime scene here and I've seen so many of them over the years. But this cheapo mask is far too tight and the swimming goggles aren't exactly cutting it.

And there's something really fuckin' weird about being in a lift while wearing all this shite. It's like you can hear yourself thinking. And you're not thinking anything good.

And the half of the shower curtain Elvis has wrapped around himself makes him look like a right daft bastard. Suspect I look as bad.

Keep checking my bum bag is still there. Aye.

The lift pings open.

'Back in a sec.' Elvis scoots out and fuck knows where he's gone.

Leaving me with Art Oscar and he's really struggling. Thing they don't tell you about some heart attacks is they just fuckin' go on and on. That third aspirin he's chomping won't save his life, but might prevent him getting too bad.

'You okay, buddy?' Hope he can hear me through the mask.

He's maybe not gurning as badly. Just clenching his jaw. 'I ain't got health insurance.'

Fuck is wrong with this country? 'If you—'

'Buddy, I'll be bankrupt if you—' Another chomp and he screws his eyes tight.

'If we don't take you, you'll be dead.' I wrap his arm over my shoulder and step out into the foyer.

Christ, the place is empty. Not exactly a fancy hotel, but it was supposed to have someone working.

At least the front door's still working, sliding open to the empty street outside, then back shut again. Nobody there, so must be a plastic bag or something triggering it.

So. That's our goal. Baby steps.

'My old boy had a heart attack about fifteen years back. Managed to save his life. I'm not letting you die. Okay?'

But Art's beyond chat right now. Just taking each tiny wee step as it comes. Pretty soon we're at the door and it swooshes *Star Trek*-style. The cold air hits my face and it's like being home. That perfect temperature. Don't realise how much I've missed the old country. 'Almost there, chief.'

I help him outside and where the fuck is everybody? The way that boy was talking on the telly, I was expecting rioting and scenes from a zombie film, but it's just dead, no undead. The sky's bright blue, not a single cloud. Actually, perfect day to film a zombie film. Nobody around.

Where's Elvis?

What's going on? Where is he? Why am I here and not at the airport and trying to get out of this country and—

Shhhh, that's the panic talking. Feeling enclosed by the mask and the goggles as much as anything.

Just breathe. Slow.

Focus on what you can see.

A homeless boy pushing a shopping cart along. Looks like that Happy Jack lad back in Edinburgh, different sides of the same coin. Or the same side of different coins.

A car rushes past, motorway speed in a quiet street.

And still no fuckin' sign of Elvis. Cheeky fucker's just left me with this clown, hasn't he?

But hold on a fuckin' minute. What if this isn't a heart attack? I mean, the boy's over twenty stone or I'm a fuckin' Dutchman, so I just assumed it was a heart attack. All the signs of one.

But that cough.

And this fuckin' country.

Mind of someone saying America's fucked because you need health insurance and you get that through your job and if you're not working, you're not covered, so people are working with this bug and what if it's not just a bad flu? What if it's a fucking killer like they say?

What if this boy has the bug?

I'm covered head to toe in what the old lady calls PPE. Personal Protective Equipment. I mean, what's wrong with calling it safety gear? Half a shower curtain, swimming goggles, rubber gloves we swiped off the housekeeper's trolley and some sex masks Elvis thought I didn't see him buying in New Orleans.

What if that's not enough?

What if his germs are already everywhere and I'm infected too?

Fuck sake, I'm forty-five and a wee bit overweight. Drink like a fuckin' fish too. Am I going to fuckin' die?

'Christ, who's the ill one?' Elvis joins us out on the street, pushing a luggage cart. 'Saw this bad boy when we checked in.'

'What the hell are you playing at?'

He eases Art down into it and it's not a pretty sight, I tell you, he just collapses into it. 'You don't look good, Bri.'

'I'm fine.' But I have to adjust my mask to try and get rid of all this condensation. Sweating like a pig here.

'No, you're panicking. It's okay.'

'Think he's got the bug?'

'Maybe. Either way, we're getting him to the hospital.' Elvis starts rummaging in Art's trouser pockets like a filthy pervert, then produces a pair of keys for one of those cheapo Chinese motors. Didn't even know they had them over here. Decent enough cars, way I hear it. He grabs the handles on the wheelchair and pushes Art along the street, and I follow them.

Takes a lot of heat from the powers that be, does old Elvis, but he's resourceful as fuck.

Aside from that wind, the thing that hits you about New York is the fuckin' size of everything. Keep forgetting Manhattan's an island, and they've crammed so fuckin' much in here.

This place looks the same in all directions, old buildings a couple of storeys tall and big fuckin' towers. Have to say, I expected Hell's Kitchen to be a bit more iconic, but it's just like fuckin' London. And nowhere should be like fuckin' London.

Those glassy buildings above us are brand new, same as the ones on the street behind us. And up ahead. So, all around us, though at least ahead you can see the water. The Hudson or the East River, fuck knows, but you know where you are with water, right?

And the other thing you normally notice about this hellhole of a city is how fuckin' busy it is. Should be a gazillion arseholes walking around like they're important, but it's empty.

Fuck, I've made a really big mistake here. Telling Elvis it was going to be fine, kidding myself it was, running away from all that shite back home, when the truth is the world's ending and we're stuck thousands of miles from home. With this fat bastard who's either dying of a heart attack, or dying of this bug and infecting us both.

This is completely fucked.

Elvis is holding his hand up like he's at the fuckin' opera and signalling to the orchestra that they're nearing the end of a movement in a Puccini. 'This way.' He sets off diagonally across the junction, pushing the wheelchair and the fat boy, heading towards a single-storey row of shops. A bank and a deli and that Chinese restaurant we dined in last night.

Almost have to jog to keep up. 'Where we going?'

But I see it before he can answer. One of those electric Toyotas parked in front of the bank, the only car on the block pretty much, and its lights flash.

'Got this.' I snatch the keys out of his hands and jog over to the car. Open the back door and—

FUCK.

It hits me.

This boy's sick as fuck and he's been driving around in this thing for fuckin' days, coughing and coughing and coughing. If he's got the bug, all this rudimentary gear isn't going to do shite against it.

'Elvis, we can't go in this thing. We'll fuckin' catch the bug.'

He looks around, but his sigh puffs his mask up. Purple with pink frilly edges, and chalk-yellow writing: "Bedside Manner". And mine is even fuckin' worse, but I'm not saying what's on it. 'He's going to die, though, Bri.'

'Not on my fuckin' watch.' I check down the street. 'It's six blocks that way, aye?'

'Something like that. But these are long blocks, Bri. Looooong blocks.'

'Fuck.'

A car pulls up behind us and this boy gets out, wearing gloves and a mask and all that shite, much better than our sex-shop shenanigans. Another hipster type, his facemask barely covering his thick beard. I mean, I've dabbled with the old facial hair over the years, but what is it with these boys and following fashion like that? Wankers. But this shitehawk's peering into Art's wagon.

I step over to the prick. 'Ho, what's up?'

He looks at us like I've just wiped my arse with his facemask and snapped it back on. 'Step back, dude.' He lifts his arms up and he's lugging two massive bags, filled with beer cans by the looks of it.

'Are you Art's mate?'

'I know Art, sure. Supposed to drop off some beer.'

I nod over at the boy. 'Listen, he's not doing too well. Any chance you could drop us at the hospital?'

Boy's doing that thing where you're like looking in two directions at the same time but not looking at either. 'Look, I'm on the clock here. I gotta work.'

'Travis, right?'

The hipster boy is stuffing his beer into the boot and he looks round at me. 'Sure.'

'So if we give you twenty-five bucks, you'll drive us there?'

'Sure thing. Call me Mo.'

And I suppose I can maybe see some Middle Eastern ancestry in the boy. Fuckin' weird how the big beards and stupid long fringes make everyone look the same, no matter where they're from originally. One big melting pot and all that. The future is hipster.

Have to help Elvis get Art in the back. Christ, we need a forklift here. I take his right arm and right leg. 'On three. One, two—'

'Are we lifting on three or is it three and lift?'

'Whatever.'

'Well, it's one or the other, Bri.'

'Just fuckin' lift! Now!'

'Fine!'

I heave the big bastard up and he weighs a fuckin' ton and CHRIST I almost tip over and Art's bum cheeks press against my mask. Sweaty, greasy arse against my fuckin' skin. Another push and he's in the back.

'Fuck sake!' I open Mo's passenger door and there's a fuckin' steering fuckin' wheel there.

THIS FUCKIN' COUNTRY.

So I get round the other side and Elvis is trying to get in the front. 'No fuckin' way!' I push the prick back and get in.

Fuckin' fuming here, I tell you.

Mo gets behind the wheel and drives off. This thing barely makes a sound. Expect it to take off any time soon. Fuckin' hell, it's like being in that film with Harrison Ford, *Blade Runner* or whatever it's called.

I sit back and just want to tear my mask off but fuck that for a game of soldiers. 'Thanks for giving us the lift, pal.'

7

CULLEN

Cullen got out of the pool car. The rain was battering down, but the covered walkway shielded him from the worst of it.

Angela wasn't so lucky, getting out into the teeming rain on her side. She darted round to his and was soaked again in seconds. 'So what did Methven say?'

'He got called away.' Cullen was trying to take in the scene. The hospital's gleaming white exterior was dampened by the Scottish rain, travelling at an almost-horizontal angle, squalling in the harsh wind. 'Which is why we're here.' He made to set off towards the prison van, all the doors opened and man-marked by three uniforms. A suited arse pressed against the nearest window.

Angela blocked his progress. 'So you didn't pick it up with him afterwards?'

Cullen knew he wasn't getting past her. 'Okay, so maybe I did.'

'And?'

He paused for a few seconds, drawing it out. But her frown was turning into a scowl. 'Angela, you're now an Acting DS.'

'Bullshit.'

'Nope.' Cullen used her confusion to barge past.

The arse in the window was replaced by a masked face, but

there wasn't that much difference. James Anderson, the lead SOCO, the top edge of his thin goatee just visible through his goggles. He made eye contact with Cullen and looked away.

Cullen caught the attention of the female uniform manning the entry. 'What's the skinny?'

'The *skinny*?' The uniform fiddled with her protective face-mask, enough for Cullen to catch her eye roll. 'A guard got stabbed, the other's head got used as a football. Luckily they're here so they're inside in A&E.' She looked them up and down. 'And if you want in the van, you'll need to suit up.'

'Right.' Cullen popped his lips a few times. 'Sergeant, can you have a look inside the van? I'll head up to the ward.' He walked off through the rain.

But Angela ran after him and rounded him. 'Are you serious? I'm an Acting DS?'

'Deadly serious. Congratulations.'

∼

THE EDINBURGH ROYAL Infirmary's Accident and Emergency department was like one of those ships found drifting at sea. The flipside of a world struggling with a pandemic was that people kept away from hospitals for anything that wasn't needing to be on a ventilator. And that'd have a cost further down the line. All those heart attacks, missed cancer treatments and—

'Can I help you?'

Cullen swung round.

'Well, well, well.' Dr Helen Yule stood in a doorway, shaking her head. Arms folded over her green scrubs, glasses dangling from her neck. Half of her right eyebrow was missing, an old scar intersecting it. 'Scott Cullen, as I live and breathe.'

'Hi Helen. Looking to speak to the guard who—'

'They just *had* to send *you*, didn't they?'

Cullen ran a hand through his hair, then put his mask back on. 'No need to be like that.'

'Really?' She jabbed a finger at the scar bisecting her eyebrow. 'This was *your* fault, Scott.'

'And there's no upper limit to how many times I can apologise, or how profusely. I'm genuinely sorry, Helen. It was my fault and if I could undo it, I would. You trusted me and I let you down. I'm sorry.'

She shook her head, but it seemed to get through to her. 'Why are you here, Constable?'

'It's Inspector now.'

'O-kay.'

'The prison guards atta—'

'Well, Officer Gilchrist is in surgery just now. It's one of those where you might be better taking it up with Prof Deeley.'

'That bad?'

'Just missed his heart.'

'And he was stabbed?'

'Right.' She touched a finger to her eyebrow. 'And the other guard, Carl Kelleher, he's with one of the nurses just now.'

'How bad is he?'

'He's fine. Ish. He was kicked in the head. We're just assessing the level of concussion. He's the type who wants to play on.'

'Still a Hibee, then?'

She smiled. 'For my sins.'

'Can I speak to him?'

She nodded slowly. 'I don't suppose I have any choice, do I?'

'Thanks, Helen.'

'Come back in ten minutes.' Her eyes creased through the goggles, showing a trace of humour. 'After you've been tested.'

'What for?'

'For Covid-19, Scott. Your old partner in crime, Craig Hunter, is upstairs getting tested just now. While it's all well and good wearing a mask, I still expect you to get a test, otherwise you'll be infecting all and sundry.'

CULLEN LEANED BACK AS FAR as he could and then tried to push back even further, but she still stuck the swab up his nose and down the back of his throat. Like an ice lolly stick being shoved into his brain. And it tickled like he was going to be sick.

And then it was done and his gag reflex was under control.

The nurse – Apinya, according to her name badge – stuck the swab into the bag. Her ancestors were from somewhere in south-east Asia, most probably Thailand, but her accent was very clearly West Lothian. And even with a mask on, she was stunning, like she should be a model rather than a nurse on the Covid-19 ward. 'Okay, that's you done.'

'Do I need to self-isolate?'

Apinya looked down at her sheet and pursed her lips. 'Well, the contact tracing form says you weren't in direct contact with the subject.'

'Correct. I wore a mask at all times too.'

'But DC Hunter didn't?'

Cullen knew that was going to come back and bite him. 'Fights are dynamic situations and I believe DC Hunter's assailant must've ripped it off.'

'Well.' She clicked her tongue a few times. 'Here's the thing. You don't need to self-isolate unless you present with symptoms.'

It hit Cullen in the gut. His whole life was built around his job, about going out into the community to help people. And being stuck at home, watching Netflix while idiots like Keith Ross torched phone masts or infected cops? That didn't sit right. Like a second punch in the balls.

Apinya was still frowning. 'Listen, I need to run this past my supervisor, okay?'

'Sure thing.' Cullen smiled at her. 'Any chance I can speak to Craig?'

'Follow me.' She led Cullen over to an internal window, keeping her two-metre distance all the way, and it was like visiting someone in prison.

A glass barrier sat between normality and someone's personal torment. Hunter was sitting on a hospital bed, slumped forward, head in his hands.

'I'll be back in a minute.' Apinya gave Cullen a flash of her eyebrows as she walked off.

Cullen picked up a handset with a gloved hand and kept it away from his head. 'Hey, Craig.'

Hunter frowned at him. 'Scott? You okay?'

'Hopefully. Just had a test. Hoping I won't have to self-isolate.'

'I will.' Hunter slumped back on the bed. 'The nurse told me... Christ, a whole load of things. Bottom line, I've got to stay at home for seven days.' His voice sounded thin and distant.

'Seven?' Cullen couldn't handle seven hours at home, let alone seven days. Didn't bear thinking about.

'I know.' Hunter sat up, rasping a hand through his hair. 'That's how long the tests are taking. If I'm not symptomatic by then, I should be fine.' He rubbed at his throat and it was like he could still taste the spit. 'Barely any point in running them, is there?'

'Have you told Chantal?'

Hunter rubbed a hand across his neck. 'Working up to it.'

'That won't be easy.'

'No. I won't be able to stay in the same flat as her. Don't want to expose her. She's fit and healthy but I'm not risking her catching it.'

'You shouldn't. Can you stay with your brother?'

Hunter shook his head. 'Murray's away again, stuck in Kenya or something. And our useless twat of a dad is house-sitting. So I'd better avoid contaminating the old pervert as well.'

'What about your mum?'

'Same rules, mate. Her immune system is shagged.' He grimaced. 'I'll have to go to a hotel. Might end up being Happy Jack's fourth wife.'

Cullen laughed. 'He'll be lucky to keep any of the others.'

'True.'

'Look, you can take my flat. It's yours, anyway. I'm just subletting it.'

'We really need to switch the lease over, don't we?'

'I mean it, Craig. Stay there.'

'But what about you?'

Cullen scratched his neck. 'I've got options, mate.'

'Like what? Yvonne?'

'Scott?' Apinya was back, clutching a sheet of paper.

Cullen smiled at Hunter. 'I'll catch you later, mate. And seriously, I'll grab a bag of clothes so you can head to your old place.'

'Thanks, Scott.'

With a final nod, Cullen replaced the handset and walked back to Apinya's station. 'So?'

'You're *sure* you wore a mask?'

'It was a standard-issue cloth mask and, yes, all the time.' Cullen was nodding like a kid on his best behaviour in the run-up to Christmas, but he couldn't help himself. 'And the suspect went in the other car, which I didn't enter.' He sighed as the truth hit him. 'And we interviewed him at the station. I'm not even sure he's got Covid-19.'

'Okay.' Apinya smiled. 'Well, the good news is we don't think you have to self-isolate, but you do need to keep that mask on and monitor your symptoms, okay?'

DR YULE STOOD in the corner, arms folded like she didn't trust Cullen. And with good reason too. But she did trust Methven and only had eyes for him. 'This is what happens when public services are underfunded. Fewer prison guards means greater risk of incidents like this. Meaning I've lost two beds to avoidable injuries.'

'You're preaching to the converted, Helen.' Methven did his eyes shut thing. 'Listen, I'm chairing a recovery meeting with the prison service and the local policing superintendent about getting the escapees back where they belong. I'll make sure your voice is heard, so they appreciate the downstream impacts.'

'Thanks, Colin. You're one of the best.'

Cullen wanted to throw up. 'Have you got a name for the other inmate yet?'

Methven shook his head. 'Paperwork issues and a lockdown at HMP Edinburgh.'

'Great. Do you mind if I have a word with Mr Kelleher?'

Yule nodded slowly. 'Be my guest.'

Christ. Cullen didn't realise that he just needed Methven's presence to deflect her. 'I mean, is it okay?'

'Sure. I'm going to rewire his jaw, but he's perfectly lucid just now.'

'Thanks.' Cullen pulled the curtain back, stepped in and sat alongside the bed.

Carl Kelleher put a finger to his temple and immediately yanked it away. He was all PPEed up, facemask and gloves. His skin was purple with bruises everywhere and his head looked like it'd been made from clay. And something had gone *very* wrong in the kiln.

He smiled at Cullen and it looked like it really hurt. 'You and me are the same, eh? Both bosses. In there, I'm a supervising officer, in charge of – *ow* – five laddies. Some good guys, some dafties. Sure it's the same in the police.'

Cullen nodded. 'Pretty much.'

'Well, the big jobbie floating in the shallow end right now is that half my bloody team are pussies. Using this whole thing as an excuse to go off on the poke.'

Cullen had seen this guy's type, alright. Acting the hero to everyone, and he was the most put-upon guy in the world. And so easy to play like a fiddle. 'Meaning you had to step in, right?'

'Right. I mean, three guys are off sick and the wing's under lockdown.' Kelleher fiddled with the strap, pulling his ear out wide. 'This isn't in the papers, but we've had ten infections. Someone brought it in and that bug's staying. So we've got to bring them in here, give them the best care blah blah blah. After what some of these boys have done?' He laughed. 'Give me a break.'

Not only did he have a hero complex, but Kelleher had let a promotion away from the shop floor turn into rust. He'd let himself go sloppy, probably over-delegated to his staff too. Cullen constantly worried that rank would do that to him, which probably meant it was unlikely to be true. Didn't stop those late-night thoughts creeping into his head, though.

'Okay, so our priority here is tracking down the prisoners.

Fastest way to do that is to speak to their known associates, family, you know the drill. Good thing is that, because they're prisoners, we'll have a lot of information on them. We can speak to the arresting officers, all that good stuff. So. You got their names?'

'Paperwork's in the van.'

'We found nothing.'

'Crap, they must've taken it.' Kelleher frowned. 'Only thing is, I don't know who one of them was.'

'What?'

'Dude, it's not my fault.'

'Not saying it is.' Cullen tried to hide his disappointment. A mystery missing prisoner wasn't going to be much fun. 'Just tell me what happened?'

'We were just about to leave when Davie, David Gilchrist, came over with the unknown prisoner. The other lad was already with me.'

'We couldn't find any paperwork.'

'Ah, crap. How's Davie doing?'

'He's in surgery, sir.'

'Heard he was stabbed. Christ.'

'Any idea who did it or how they got a knife?'

'That little shite.' He bared his teeth. 'The lad I was looking after is called Kenjo in there, but his Sunday name is Kenny Falconer.'

Cullen felt himself groan. He wouldn't have to look far for the arresting officer. It was himself.

8

BAIN

And just like fuckin' that, the traffic appears. Mo has to pull up behind a wave of arseholes in *all* the cars. And they're fuckin' massive over here. Aside from the electric things like Mo here's driving, they've got these tanks that pretend to be cars. The kind of shite Elvis was keen on hiring down in Texas. And they're all petrol, so they must burn through the fuel like Art through cheesecake. Or me through a box of IPA, in fairness.

I swivel round and the boy's looking not too shabby, considering he's fuckin' dying here. 'Won't be long, pal.'

'He's not got long, Bri.' Elvis has that look of the piss artist caught mid-session with some earth-shattering event, struggling to sober up but too far gone and is just ... lost. 'Any shortcuts round here, Mo?'

'Sorry, man. This is New York.'

'Be quicker walking...'

Mo grins at him in the rearview. 'I'd agree with you, if you hadn't left the wheelchair back there.' He pulls forward, drumming his thumbs off the steering wheel in time to that band I like but can't remember the name of. 'Won't be too long, man.'

'Who's this?'

Mo looks at us with this big grin. 'The War On Drugs.'

Makes us nod. 'That's who it is...'

'You a fan?'

'Quite like them, aye. Prefer Kurt Vile's solo stuff, but hey ho.'

'Huh.' Mo pulls forward almost at the junction now. 'Just two blocks to go.' And we're almost through, but a homeless guy runs across the crosswalk. Mo slams on the brakes and we all jerk forward. 'Goddamnit!'

The tramp batters the bonnet with both fists, then points at Mo for a good few seconds, tongue out and waggling in the air. Then he scurries off to the pavement.

'Goddamn asshole.' Mo's torn his seatbelt off and is out of the car. 'Hey, asshat! Get back here!' And just like that, he's off, chasing after the guy down some fuckin' street in Manhattan. Christ.

I take one look at Elvis, then at Art. 'We are *fucked*.'

'Bri, he's left his keys.'

And holy crapballs, Elvis is right. A big metal star ring is dangling from the ignition thingy. A ton of keys on there, like he's a jailer.

Even so, I shake my head. 'We can't take his car.'

'Aye we can.'

'That's grand theft auto!'

'Aye, and Art's going to die here!'

Another check and, fuck me, Mo's number is printed on a bit of card stuck to the dashboard. No sign of his phone either. Usually those fannies have them in cradles on the dashboard, but his must be in his pocket. Must've taken it. So we can borrow his motor and get it back to him. 'Fuck this for a game of soldiers.' I shuffle over to the driver side and fuck me is it a tight fit.

'Need to cut down on your pork life.' Art's staring at me, lucid now.

'Those in glass houses, pal.' I shove the seat back.

'Ow!' Art's glaring at us.

'Sorry, pal.' I stick the car in drive and – OH MY FUCKIN' DAYS – I've got a green light, so I floor it and whizz across the junction onto the next block.

The traffic's backed up at the end but I've got a clear run at it. Must be three or four blocks now.

I check in the back. Elvis and Art are both looking to the side. Is that where the hospital is? 'Everyone okay—'

'Stop!' Elvis's peepers are almost out on stalks.

I slam the brakes and we squeal to a stop.

An ambulance is sitting there, blocking the road. The back doors are hanging open. The two paramedics are getting a fuckin' shoeing off a gang of kids. Looks like a ton of them, too, swarming the van in sheer numbers with fists. One hits a paramedic and he swings round to chase, but another hits from behind. Rinse and repeat.

And fuck me, there's a couple of the wee toerags raiding the back of the van.

'Fuck sake.' I undo my belt and get out into the cold.

And Elvis is with me on the pavement. 'Bri, this is New York. These boys are always armed.'

Another scan and all I see is fists and purple T-shirts. Boys of all colours and most sizes, just no real fat bastards in there. 'I don't see anyone armed. Come on.' Fists clenched, I walk over to the ambulance. 'Hey, cunts! You want to try handling some Glasgow steel?'

Not that any of the pricks take any notice. This big lanky streak of piss lands one on the paramedic and pushes him over. Real nasty-looking fucker, too, skinhead and a trimmed beard. Big stupid ears. He's laying the boot in, and his two mates are standing back, pair of big rugby types pulling the other medic away.

Makes me think this cunt is the ringleader.

So fuck it, I head straight for him and elbow his mates out of the way. Pair of them go down like a sack of spuds. Them out of the way, I take another step over to the boy and stick the fuckin' nut on him.

Crunch, right in the middle of his nose.

He stumbles back into the ambulance, his hands all over his nose, trying to stop the blood pishing out. Boy's fingers are covered in sovvy rings, though, so I better be careful here. I take a swing at this prick's plums, but I miss and just catch him on the thigh.

My bonce is fuckin' screaming at us to stop, but fuck this, I'm on him, lashing out with fists and trying to stick the nut on again, but some cunt's pulling me back and it better not fuckin' be Elvis, only it's not just one cunt it's about twenty and it's like being at a gig where we're all crushed in together and I can't fuckin' breathe and they're pushing and pulling us at the same time and it's just fuckin' dirty hands all over my body and they've got my fuckin' mask and my goggles and the fuckin' shower curtain's over my fuckin' head and I can't fuckin' see anything and some cunt punches me in the kidneys.

And I'm on my knees now inside the ambulance somehow.

And my back is fuckin' sore. Really fuckin' sore. Feels like some cunt's pulled out my spine and put it back in the wrong way round. I try to get up but someone smacks us in the chops. My skin feels raw from it.

'Don't mess with us, bitch!'

Loud footsteps heading away from us. Scummy little fuckers, stealing from a fuckin' ambulance. I mean... Talk about low.

I haul the shower curtain over my head and chuck it to the side, then step back outside the ambulance.

Elvis is on the ground, and they've stripped him. Just his underpants sparing his modesty. And his sex mask. His clothes are everywhere, but it's like a path leading to those cunts.

The paramedics are getting up. Boys look fucked, likes. Battered and bruised.

'Stay with him.' I set off away from them, pounding my feet off the pavement and starting to pick up the pace like when I ran cross country at school, then at training college and I'm getting into a groove and getting faster and faster and feeling strong as a fuckin' ox and there they fuckin' are!

Daft cunts are all wearing pinks and purples. The fuck is that all about?

'Come here!'

The big one, the leader, stops and looks round at us, but he fuckin' knows he's going to get battered again, so he scrams.

I shoot after him, speeding up still, but I feel a fuckin' stitch forming. Absolute bastard, like I've been stabbed in the guts again.

Half of those wee shites head into the subway, the other half into a back alley, but I've got no choice but to follow the big boy down into the fucking underground station.

Need to take it slow down the steps. Aside from not wanting to go arse over tit down them, I'm not on home turf here. No baton, no back-up, just Elvis in his grundies and a pair of smacked-in paramedics.

Into the ticket area and fuck me, there are just too many ways those boys could've gone. Train lines running everywhere on or off the island and in both directions too. And the roar of engines makes it sound like they're all leaving at the same time.

The little cunts have got away.

9
CULLEN

Angela was panting much harder than Cullen by the time they got to the fifteenth floor of the tower block. Through the window at the end, the living hell of Wester Hailes spread around them like lava from a volcano. So many miserable lives forgotten about and uncared for. The lift still being knackered was proof, if anything. And this floor was one of the worst. Been a few years since Cullen had been up here, but it only seemed to have got worse in that time.

He stepped onto the landing and sucked in a deep breath, but his recent exercise regime was paying off. Focusing on fitness instead of bulk. And he had Hunter to thank for it. He raised an eyebrow at Angela. 'Should get out running.'

'You try getting any time to yourself when you're raising two kids on your own.'

Cullen winced. 'Sorry, I keep forgetting.'

'Hard to process what happened, even after all this time.' Angela took a final deep breath, then walked over the narrow hallway to the address. 'Police!' She knocked on the door. 'Didn't we raid here a few years ago?'

'Can't remember. Been here a couple of times and it all just blends together.' Cullen looked around the place, trying to check for differences between reality and a fading memory.

'There was definitely one of those steel doors here, but I'm not sure it was this floor. Or even this building.'

'Was Kenny here last time?'

'Can't remember.' Cullen sucked in a deep breath and caught a vague whiff of something quasi-legal, at best. 'You ever run across him?'

'Eh, he punched me in the tits once, you daft sod. When I was still in uniform.'

'Christ, that takes me back. Feels like a lifetime ago.'

'Less time than you'd think.'

The door opened and a man's face peered out. Pudgy and looking ultra-stoned. The fug of dope smell backed up that theory. Ricky Falconer didn't seem to be too concerned that two cops were showing up at his door while he was wasted. 'Yo?'

'Looking for Kenny. He in?'

'Aye.'

Cullen took hold of his baton, ready to snap it out and threaten with it. 'So can we speak to him?'

'Eh?'

'You said he's in.'

'No, man, I meant he's inside. Barlinnie.' Ricky frowned. 'Or was it Saughton? Fuck knows, man.'

Angela narrowed her eyes at him. 'When was the last time you saw him?'

'Back around Christmas time.' Ricky started clicking his fingers. 'Aye, man, that was it. Me and the old lady visited him in Saughton. Her Majesty's Prison Edinburgh, eh?'

Angela glanced at Cullen, clearly thinking along the same lines, then at Ricky. 'Can we speak to your mother?'

'You a medium, doll?'

'What's my dress size got to—'

Ricky's burst of laughter cut her off. 'No, man, can you speak to the spirits?'

'She's dead?'

'Aye. Massive heart attack on New Year's Day, man. I mean, they say women don't have them, least not the same as fellies, and she was skin and bone, man, skin and bone, but she popped her clogs over a steak pie and glass of sherry. Tragic, man, tragic.'

'So your brother's not been in touch?'

'He wasn't at the funeral. My uncle Robert went in to speak to him, but he said Kenny didn't believe him that she was dead. Thought she was living in Perth with Robert.'

'And was she?'

'No, man. She's dead.' Ricky frowned, bleary-eyed, maybe sensing something was up. 'What's he done?'

'You mind if we have a look inside?'

'Nothing to hide.' Ricky stepped aside to let them in.

Cullen let Angela go first and, sure enough, Ricky had nothing to hide.

The flat was a typical bedsit, kitchen units on the walls, bare mattress in the middle of a floor littered with empty pizza boxes. An open door showed an avocado bathroom suite.

Ricky sat down and picked up a roll-up from an ashtray in the middle of the floor and sparked at a lighter. 'Come on, you banjo bastard thing.' It clicked and a flame licked at his cigarette. 'So, let me guess, he's escaped?'

'Correct in not-even-one.' Angela poked her head into the bathroom, but it didn't take long to search it. She turned to face Ricky. 'You seem to know a lot about it, though.'

Ricky took a long drag and exhaled cigarette smoke. Not even Kenny Falconer's brother would openly smoke dope in front of the cops. 'Sister, all I know is, when me and the old girl – God rest her soul – visited Kenny, he was talking about getting out. Reckoned he had a plan to get away.'

'Know what that plan was?'

'Man, I thought he's never likely to be able to carry it out, so I didn't ask. Kenjo's got a twenty-year sentence without parole, eh?'

Angela couldn't help herself from rolling her eyes. 'Well, if he will sell illegal knives and kill people...'

'Doll, I haven't heard from him in months. Besides, he still owes me a ton of backpay.'

'Backpay?'

'From his bookshop.'

Gorgie Road was eerily quiet, like this section of the city had decided to lock down before an official order. Unusual for people to follow instructions like that.

Boab's Books was somehow still trading, but it seemed to have evolved from a grotty porn shop stocking some grottier paperbacks into a hipster coffee shop stocking grotty paperbacks. Still the same *Boab's Books* sign, though, blood-red text on a black background, but it had been cleaned up and looked a deliberate style choice rather than inherited from the previous owner. Not that the owner had changed.

Angela stopped outside and grabbed Cullen's sleeve, blocking his entry. She stared at him, shaking her head. Didn't look like she was going to let go of his sleeve any time soon. 'Scott, you're lying to me.'

'I'm not!'

'All I asked is if Kenny Falconer was connected to Dean Vardy. That's it. I can handle the truth.'

'It's not just a simple thing, is it? If he was connected, what are you going to do? Push him down a flight of stairs?'

She looked away. 'No.'

'Angela, are you sure you want to know?'

She didn't think about it. 'I'm sure.'

'Okay, so he supplied knives for Dean Vardy's outfit. We could never prove it, mind, but we can track at least five murders from Vardy's goons to Falconer's knives.'

She looked up at the sky. 'Thanks.'

'You okay?'

'Let's do this.' She stepped through the door and got a really nice chiming sound.

Cullen followed her in. The coffee smell was gorgeous.

'Gagging for one, like.' Angela marched up to the counter.

Behind the till, a blackboard had yellow letters clicked into place, advertising the various ways the barista could add hot liquids to ground coffee beans.

What the hell was a V60, anyway?

And cold-brewed coffee? People still drank that?

'With you in a second.' The hipster barista was pouring hot water from an ancient brass kettle into a filter cone, and taking his bloody time with it too. He looked like he'd walked straight off the cover of the *Gothamite* magazine, maybe a semi-ironic Art Oscar piece on non-toxic masculinity. Braces, checked shirt rolled up to the elbows to show off sleeve tattoos that stretched down the backs of his hands. Chunky specs and a long beard that was surely a magnet for a particular coronavirus.

The shop was tiny, five metres square, with heaving bookshelves all over the place, tables and chairs scattered throughout. One thing hadn't changed – incense sticks still burned in empty wine bottles.

A couple of punters lugged tatty old books in stacks from their waists to their chins, matching his and hers thrillers, and dumped them on the counter.

Cullen spotted another yellow-text clicky blackboard thing:
Lockdown is coming!
Get your read on!
Clearance sale, baby!
Ten books for a fiver! Cash only.

But it looked like the only member of staff was the barista. And it wasn't obvious whose coffee he was making either. Then again, if Ricky Falconer was managing the place, then good luck to him. The male customer handed over six tenners and they eased the stacks of books outside.

Cullen walked up to the counter and held up his warrant card. 'You the manager?'

'For my sins, yeah.' London accent and posh with it. 'Call me Reginald. That's with a W.'

'Wreginald?'

'That's right.' Wreginald sipped the coffee himself, soaking his moustache whiskers with creamy foam. 'God, that's good. Can I get you one?'

'We're fine.' Cullen put his warrant card away. 'Do you know the owner?'

'Just deal with his brother. Ricky?' Wreginald shook his head. 'Some guy. I mean, I sort of rent the place from him. The books are now a sideline, but the coffee is making a *mint*. Roast it myself. If this country locks down, though...'

'So you've never met the owner?'

'Kenny. Right. Never met the chap.'

'And yet you know his name.'

Wreginald stared into his cup. 'Shit.'

'Sir, are you lying to us?'

'No!'

'Have you heard from him?'

'Nope.'

'Is he here?'

'No!' But Wreginald glanced through the back.

'He's here, isn't he?'

'No!'

Cullen walked over to the shop door and put the snib down. He nodded at Wreginald. 'Stay here. Okay? Don't leave.'

Wreginald glanced at the door, but perfect timing. A squad car pulled up and the two uniforms got out, then came into the shop.

Cullen waved at them. 'Keep him here.'

'Sure thing.' The bigger of the two nodded at Wreginald. 'Any of that cold brew left?'

Cullen didn't want to ask, didn't want to order the guy not to extort free coffee. He opened the door and entered the back corridor.

A stair led up to a half-open door. Stacks of books lay on the steps, probably ready to go out on the shelves as part of the desperate clearance sale.

Cullen drew his baton, ready to snap out with the first swing, and headed up. He stopped by the door but couldn't see anyone inside.

Angela walked up behind him, her face like a robot from the future sent to murder the mother of a resistance leader.

Cullen checked his mask was secured, then nudged the door open with his baton. Still no sounds or smells, so he sneaked in.

The room was dark, with the curtains drawn, and well-furnished, hand-made wooden kitchen units on three sides. In the middle, a leather sofa sat in front of a giant TV with a PlayStation game resting on the pause menu, a hulking Greek god flexing his ludicrous muscles.

No sign of Kenny Falconer.

'He's not here.' Cullen walked over the sofa to inspect in closer detail. The game controller was plugged into some fancy headphones, the sort his old man would wear in his man cave while rocking out to his shite old music. He walked over to the counter and rested his hand against the kettle. Cold.

A blister pack of pills sat in a cupboard, half-popped.

Cullen snapped on a pair of gloves and took them out. 'Ah, Christ. These are the same anti-5G ones Keith Ross was selling.'

Angela scowled at him. 'How could anyone be so bloody stupid?'

Something rattled behind the twitching curtains. A body. Moving. Trying to pull up the sash window.

Cullen put a finger to his lips, then eased his way over. Guy was usually armed, so one of two ways to play this. Charge and knock the wind out of him? But he was by a window and Cullen didn't need the paperwork hassle. He gave Angela the nod, then lashed out with his baton and it extended fully as it arced round. Metal cracked off bone.

Angela wrapped the curtains around the screaming figure and pulled them away from the wall with a bursting sound.

Cullen knelt on the twitching body and eased the curtains wide.

Kenny Falconer was staring up at him, his facemask covering his eyes. He coughed and it sounded like he'd torn something in his lungs. 'Man.'

Cullen grabbed his T-shirt and held him in place. 'Kenny Falconer, I'm arresting you for—'

Falconer coughed again, loud and harsh, and collapsed into a sitting position under the window. His face was close to turning purple as he did another wracking cough.

And Angela booted him in the balls. 'That's for my husband.'

10

BAIN

Ah you bastard, I'm fuckin' aching here. Legs feel like school dinner custard but even fuckin' thicker. And heavier.

And where the fuck am I? Some New York street but they all look the same round here. Hardly one of those fuckin' iconic parts of the city. *Think* I came this way, but the traffic's fucked off and it's all spooky quiet again.

Reminds me of being twatted in London that one time, no idea where I was going and I could barely see my own nose I was that pished. Still ended up back in Soho for a bunk up, mind.

And my fuckin' arse is aching too. Someone must've kicked the gluteal and it's just *ow*. My kidney too. Last thing I need is to lose my liver, but thank fuck I've got two fuckin' kidneys.

Fuck sake.

Something's clicking and rattling in my left leg, just above the hip. Is the gall bladder down there? Appendix? Or my fuckin' spleen?

No. It's my fuckin' phone in my pocket. Christ, I can't hear shite. Must've clattered me in both ears, feels like my bonce is filled with cotton wool.

I take it out and some yank number is calling us. Fuck, who is this? I put it to my ear. 'Hello?'

'You stole my fucking car, man!' Ah shite, it's Mo. And he doesn't sound happy. '*My* fucking car, man!'

'Pal, I had to. You ran off after some tramp and—'

'Where is it?'

'Eh, good question.'

He sighs down the line. 'Where did you take it?'

'Just a couple blocks, pal. Listen, I got into a swedge with some local kids who were stealing from an ambulance and—'

'Stay where you are, man. I'll come to you.'

'I would, but I've no fuckin' idea where I am now.'

'Can you see a street name?'

Can I? Fuck knows. I can't quite focus on anything. 'Haven't you got a tracker in your car?'

But he's gone.

Fuck this. I think it's just up ahead.

Wait a sec, there's red and blue lights flashing with a sprinkling of enough white to keep it patriotic.

I haul my weary fuckin' bones along the street, heading towards the light like I'm diving again and close to drowning and need to get up to the fuckin' surface. Press my thumbs and palms into my eyes and I can fuckin' see again.

Thank fuck – a cop car has turned up. Two big guys are standing with Elvis, one black and one the same sort of rosy pink that passes for white back home. The paramedics are seeing to each other, both looking pretty fucked.

Elvis waves at us. 'Brian chased them off, aye.'

The big black dude walks over to us. He's stacked, big fuckin' arms and the size of chest you only get from deadlifts. And not kettle bells either, big fuckin' dumbbells. Short sleeves in this weather, but it seems like it's to show off his tats. Big spider-y things on his right arm, and a dude playing a double bass on his left. And their uniforms here are covered in badges and embroidery and fuck knows what any of it means. Makes them look like soldiers. And he looks pretty fuckin' pissed off with us, like, but hey ho.

I thumb behind me. 'Lost them back at the underground.'

'Underground? Oh, the subway. Huh.' The dude takes a

deep breath. 'Well. Charles Holten.' He holds out a hand, grinning away. 'I'd shake, but you know how it is.'

'Too right I do.'

'Gather you're a cop?'

'Aye, pal. Chased the wee fuckers, but they just scattered and disappeared into the subway and some back alleys.'

'Figures. They're opportunists. Low-level, but it's an effective strategy for them.' Holten folds his massive arms across his chest. 'They were after N95 masks. Respirators. Real nasty business. Steal from a hospital or an ambulance, then sell on the black market. Don't know who's worse, the scumbags who steal, or the sons of bitches who buy this stuff. Upper West Side types who want to protect themselves. Hate to break it to them, but it doesn't matter shit if other people can't stop this bug spreading, or the ICU can't help you because they ain't got any masks.'

'I hear you.'

He gives a tight military nod. Maybe the magic's working and he's starting to trust us. 'Didn't get away with anything, though, so well done.'

I look over at the ambulance. 'Seriously? Nothing?'

'Uh huh. EMTs did a full inventory before they saw to each other. All the masks are still there.'

'Well, that's a relief.'

Another nod. Doesn't give much away, does he? 'They got a 911 call, said some old dude in an apartment had Covid and needed to be intubated. So they turned up, got out onto the street, and those rats just swarmed 'em.'

'Fuckin' nasty shites. Get them back home.'

'Where in Canada you from?'

'Canada?' I'm actually laughing. Hope he means it to be funny. 'Come on. I'm Scottish.'

'Huh. Got relatives in Glasgow. You know it?'

'Don't talk to me about Glasgow, pal.' But I say it with a smile.

Holten sniffs, then hands us a business card. 'Buddy, you're not on your home turf, so you give me a call if you need anything. And don't go hunting after gangs. You got lucky this time. They could've been armed.' He looks around, scowling. 'This city, man.'

'Some place, that's for sure.' The card's lovely, really thick and got this nice texture to it. I'm about to put it away when I spot Mo's car. Two big problems, rolled into one. 'Well, actually, a pal there needs to go to the hospital...'

'Sure thing.'

I lean in maybe a bit too close. 'And there's a Travis driver who needs to be calmed down a wee bit.'

'What did you do?'

'What I had to, pal.'

He laughs. 'I hear you.'

I get out my phone and fuck me, the screen's cracked. Shite, that's going to cost a fuckin' packet to fix. And I'll need to find someone to do it, too. Most of the shops are fuckin' shut. I reach for my wallet to put the card away.

But it's not there.

Ah, fuck. Those cunts stole my bum bag!

11

CULLEN

'Okay, so...' Apinya tugged at her mask like it was annoying her even more than Angela Caldwell was. She sighed then rested it back behind her ears. 'Okay, well Mr Falconer's here now.' She checked her watch again. 'Better late than never.'

Cullen folded his arms across his chest. 'I'd rather it didn't take two injured guards and another inmate on the run.'

'Well, he's not going anywhere now.'

'How is he?'

'He's tested positive for Covid-19. The prison's medical officer conducted a test last week and he was isolated in the medical ward, but his condition worsened this morning, so they were concerned that he needed medical intervention.'

Cullen felt his mask tighten around his skin. 'So he's been passing that bug on to people?'

'He was wearing a mask. No idea where he got it, presumably from Carl Kelleher, but it will have likely prevented any further spread of the novel coronavirus.'

'That's a good thing. But you're testing that barista guy?'

'Ah, you mean Donald Dunn?'

Cullen shrugged. 'Only identified to us as Wreginald. With a W.'

'That figures. I know police officers, and they know good

coffee. Wreginald brews a nice cup. I know why some people won't share information with you.'

'Charming. 'How is Wreginald?'

'*He*'s fine. Stay at home, isolate, watch for symptoms, blah blah blah. He's going to play with some new coffee recipes.'

Apinya fixed Angela with a hard stare. 'Kenny Falconer, on the other hand, keeps complaining of severe testicular pain. Any idea what caused that?'

Cullen caught Angela grinning at him, but he really needed to have a word with her about battering Falconer's balls up into his stomach. 'He must've fallen.'

'Fallen, sure. Heard that one a million times.'

'Swear it's the truth. He saying anything?'

'Not to me, no.'

'Can we speak to him?'

'Not so sure. Your problem is that he's started seeing things. Hallucination is a side effect of taking chloroquine diphosphate at such doses.' Apinya shook her head. 'Whoever's dealing those drugs... It's a crime.'

'I mean, literally, yes.' Angela walked over to the glass. 'And it's one of the reasons we need a word.'

Through the window, Kenny Falconer lay on the bed, staring at the ceiling. All his stabbing and escaping and murdering had got him nowhere but where he was supposed to be. He coughed and his whole body wracked.

Angela was frowning. 'Isn't there supposed to be a guard here?'

'Prison service sent someone, aye. But he's speaking to Mr Kelleher in A&E.'

'You know how the surgery went?'

She looked away. 'The prison guard died.'

It hit Cullen like a knee in the balls. Another murder by Kenny Falconer. Another preventable one, too. 'Mind if we just have a quick word with him?'

Apinya checked both directions. 'Okay, so I need to leave for the night. I'll get my boss to send someone over but in the meantime, can you have a look at this?' She handed Angela the handset. 'I'm not sure it's working.'

'I'll see what I can do.' Angela grinned at her.

Apinya slipped off away from them.

'Good work.' Cullen joined Angela by the window. 'But we still need to have a chat about you tanning his balls.'

'Seriously?'

'Seriously. Whatever's happened to you, whatever Falconer did to you and his mate Vardy did to Bill, you can't just hoof him in the conkers.'

Angela wasn't taking it seriously. Her face lit up like she was in the front row of a gig by that shite comedian she liked, the fat Cockney one.

'I'm being serious here. I shouldn't use words like that, sorry.'

'Fights are dynamic situations, Scott. You know that as well as I do. I was aiming for his thigh and he moved.'

'You need to at least appear to regret it.'

'Fine. I regret it.' With a sigh, Angela picked up the handset and spoke into it: 'Kenny?'

He looked over at the window, but didn't say anything.

'Can you hear me, Kenny?'

'Not talking to you.'

Angela looked like she was going to fight back, so Cullen snatched the handset from her. 'Go and stall Apinya's boss.'

'Righty-ho.' She took one last look at Falconer then trudged off away from the window.

Cullen put the handset as close to his mouth as he dared: 'Kenny, you know me, so let's cut the shite, okay? Who were you working with?'

'Nobody.'

'Don't give me that. You escaped with another prisoner. We have too much history to be playing games here. Tell me where he is.'

'You think I want to tell you anything, pal?'

'You'll get another eight years for that trick today. And that's just the escape part. You murdered a guard, Kenny.'

Falconer shrugged. The exact response Cullen expected. Taking a life with no remorse. The world must be a strange place to someone who could do that.

'That's another life sentence, Kenny. You seem intent on collecting them.'

'What was the plan? Sit this out in the flat above your bookshop?'

'I was waiting for someone. Boy who worked for Dean Vardy, owes me a favour.'

'He know you've got that bug?'

Another shrug. 'He was going to take us on a wee trip up north to see my mother.'

'Kenny, your mother's dead.'

'Bullshit.'

'It's the truth, Kenny. She died in January.'

'My uncle Robert, fucking lying bastard, man.' Falconer slumped back in the bed with another wracking cough. Five or six in quick succession.

'Where did you get the pills?'

'They're to help me.'

'Who gave you them?'

'What's it to you?'

'Was it Wreginald?'

'No.'

'Kenny, they're poisoning you. Worse than whatever bug you've got, if you've even got one. These fits and coughs and whatever else, it's because your body's receiving toxic shock.'

'So?'

'How many did you take?'

'Not telling you that. Got them inside.'

'So you want to die?'

'What?'

'You're happy to die in a hospital bed of poisoning from a stupid drug? Rather than face prison like a man.'

'You should try it, pal. Wouldn't even last a day in there.'

'You're probably right. I'm a cop. But then, some people are better inside than out. I respect you for who you are, Kenny, and what you can do.' Cullen left a pause and waited for a reaction. There, a slight curling of the lips. 'But that respect has to cut both ways, Kenny. I'm not going to talk shite to you and I am sincerely sorry to have to tell you about your mother. I love my mum too, mate, so I can't imagine...'

Kenny lay there, blinking.

'The way I see it, Kenny, you were the brains behind your escape attempt. You've got the muscle to pull it off. Right?'

'Maybe.'

'What did your mate contribute? A smile? A knowing wink?'

And he'd lost him. Back to staring up at the ceiling.

'What could the other guy have contributed, Kenny? Wait, I see it, you're the total package, right? Brains, brawn, skill. Contacts. Even got some money.'

Still nothing. Not even the faint smile.

Sod it. 'Your mate must be a coward, right?'

Kenny looked over, frowning. 'Eh?'

'Well, it's that or he's using you. Either way, he's preying off your strength and skills to get out of prison.'

'Nah, Kegsy's alright, mate.'

Got you.

Cullen smiled at him. 'Kegsy, eh?'

Falconer slumped back in the bed. 'Ah fuck.'

Cullen had no idea who Kegsy was. But someone at the prison would know.

12

BAIN

'I mean...' I watch New York whizz past. Up ahead, the ambulance weaves in traffic behind Holten's car, carrying Art Oscar to safety. 'And who fuckin' steals a wallet but leaves a phone?'

'You expecting me to show you some sympathy here?' Mo's shaking his head as he drives, but he seems to love this, getting escorted by two of New York's finest through Downtown Manhattan. 'You *stole* my car, man.'

Actually, I've no idea what "Downtown" means. Always think I do, then someone fuckin' bursts it open wide.

'I did what I had to. You ran off after that tramp and we needed to get laughing boy to hospital.'

In the back, Elvis is looking fucked. Head between his knees, fingers clawing at his hair.

'Mm.' Mo pulls out to follow Holten's motor through a particularly snarled up section. 'You want to know?'

'Enlighten me.'

'Because the cops can track a cellphone. Can't track a wallet.'

'I can track mine.' Elvis is upright and leaning forward. 'Got a little tracker thing in it.'

'That only works locally, dumbass.'

I shoot a glower at Mo. 'You got rage issues or something?'

Mo looks over at us. 'Like you don't?'
I just try and shrug it off. 'What's "Downtown" mean?'
'Downtown?'
'Aye, what's it mean?'
'Downtown is... Downtown. It just is what it is.'
'I know, but where is it?'
'It's where... Like the businesses are. And like bus and subway stations. Galleries and the Federal Building and City Hall and—'
'But that's all over New York?'
'Right, but it's just... Downtown. Where everything is.'
'You mean the high street?'
'The what?'
Fuck sake. Two cultures divided by a common language... 'The city centre?'
Mo grins. 'I guess.'
'Why not just say "city centre" then? Why Downtown?'
'Well, we've Midtown and Uptown too. And don't get me started on Chinatown and The Village.'
'Some people say it's from Boston.' Elvis is back between us, got his phone out. His seems to have escaped being smashed by twats. 'But Wikipedia says it comes from this fine city. Early nineteenth century, there was a town at the southern edge of the island of Manhattan.' He thumbs behind us, but I don't think south's that way. 'That's where all the business stuff was at the time. Only way to grow was north, or up if you're looking at a map. And that was all houses.'
'Huh.' Mo shrugs. 'Never knew that.'
'And Elvis here knows bugger all except how to use that phone of his.'
'You're lucky you've got me, Bri.'
Judging by the signs and stuff, we're like a block away from the hospital. Not that it's that much different from back the way. Just more Starbucks and better-looking delis. And one of those tunnel things over the pavement you see on films too, but it's for a bar rather than a swanky hotel. Probably a smoking shelter. Fuckin' Irish pub, too. I mean, I like the Irish as much as the

next man, but Guinness is an average beer at best. Much better stouts out there.

'You're lucky I'm not pressing charges.'

'I'm not lucky, I've just got a new buddy in the NYPD. And you're lucky you're not getting done for attempted murder. Running off like that, you twat.'

'Dude was asking for it.'

'You catch him?'

'Nope.' Mo pulls up on the right. Row of trees on the pavement, all starting to come out green. 'Here we are.'

Big pink building with glass in the middle. Twenty floors maybe. Looks like a fancy hotel.

'This is the hospital?'

'Sure is. What were you expecting?'

'Don't know, but not that.'

'Well. You can get out now. And don't forget to five star me.'

'Sure thing.' I get out onto the street and the wind hits me again. I mean, it's nothing like back home but it's got something unique to this country, I tell you.

Mo drives off into the traffic with a wave.

Fuck it, I give the boy a four. Or at least it looks like that through the cracks.

Elvis claps my arms. 'So, what's the plan now?'

'Get tested, I suppose.' Hate to think about going on a ventilator, but better to know, right? 'Those pricks nicked our shower curtains and... Elvis, we need to talk about those sex masks.'

'Come on, Bri. You said you weren't going to mention them again.'

'What happens in the safety of your own bedroom between you and Danielle is sacrosanct. I just dislike having to wear her mask.'

'It's just that you've got a much bigger head than me.'

And the phone rings. The little lady. 'Hey, what's up?'

'Brian, someone's stolen my car! Outside work!'

'Shite. Have you called it in?'

'Of course. What the hell—'

'Look, I can't help. I'm sorry, but I'm stuck here. Please, call it in. They'll send someone round and—'

'I need to get home to Mum. She's with your dad and they've got—'

'Okay, okay. Get a taxi. Call the cops, get a crime number and tell them I've instructed you on this, okay? Use my name and rank. Then call your mum. And call me when you get in the taxi, okay?'

'Okay.' She sounds a lot calmer. Christ, it's so good just hearing her voice. 'I better go.'

'Love you.' I end the call and sit back.

Christ. On top of everything else.

Elvis pats us on the arm. 'Come on, Bri, let's get those tests.'

13

CULLEN

Cullen powered along the road, racing the tram as it headed through the west Edinburgh badlands on its way to the airport. Seemed unusually quiet today and, there you go, it slowed to pull in at the next stop, so he won.

Then his phone blasted out through the dashboard speakers. Shabba Ranks, *Mr Loverman*. Supposed to be ironic, but he couldn't get it to bloody stop.

Angela was sitting in the passenger seat, arms folded and shaking her head at him, but she was grinning like an idiot on super-strong ecstasy, mouthing along to the "Mr Loverman" and "Shabba" lines. 'Pull in and answer it, then.'

Cullen pulled in to the prison car park, then stopped. He neither wanted to bounce Evie's call or have Angela listen in to it. 'Can you go and park it?'

'Sure thing, Shabba.'

'Thought it was on silent.' Cullen opened his door and grabbed his phone. He got out, leaving the engine running, and let Angela pass him, humming the tune's melody. He stepped back and Angela raced across towards the prison car park.

Cullen walked over to the low bollards guarding the prison's entrance and answered it.

Evie was still there. 'Bothering to pick up then?'

'Long story.'

'Oh, Scott.'

'You got my text, then?'

'Would rather find out by a phone call than text that my supposed boyfriend had endangered himself by taking someone down solo, especially if that someone might've had Covid.'

'Supposed?'

'That's the bit you're focusing on?'

'Look, I tried calling, but you didn't answer.'

'Right. Sorry, I've been busy too.'

Cullen scanned the car park for Angela, trying to work out how long he had before she came over to listen in. The wrong words and he'd be living it down for months, if not years. That song was going to remain long in the memory. 'Evie, times are tough. I'm back in bloody uniform.' He stared down at the black material, slightly too big for a change. 'You know how many people are off sick? I've lost Lauren Reid already, and Craig Hunter's self-isolating.'

'What?'

'He was the one who took him down on that roof.'

'Took who down? What roof?'

Shite. He hadn't told her about Keith Ross. Just Kenny Falconer. 'Never mind.'

'You went up on a rooftop without back-up?'

'They were burning a phone mast!'

'*Still.*'

'Who told you?'

'That's not important.'

'Lennox, wasn't it?'

'Maybe. But you were playing cowboy again, Scott. We've had this discussion.'

'It was necessary.'

'Maybe once, but you've been at it twice now.'

'We caught him.'

'And the ends justify the means?'

'Look, Kenny wore a mask and we didn't get *that* close to him. It was fine. Stupid arsehole was taking this anti-5G pill he'd got inside and—'

'*Christ*, Scott.' Evie let out a long sigh. Still no sign of Angela walking over. 'I really like you, but you're such a stupid bastard at times.'

'I'm my own worst enemy, I know.'

'Have you been tested?'

'I have, but it's still probably too early. Something about pre-symptomatic versus asymptomatic.'

'Can never be too early.'

'Well, you can, but I know what you mean.' And he spotted Angela heading over. He needed to hit her now. 'So, you know how I mentioned Craig self-isolating?'

Evie groaned. 'Because he can't be in the same place as Chantal, you've offered him your flat?'

'Right. How did you guess?'

'Don't pretend that you're not extremely transparent, Scott. This is your way of saying you want to stay at mine, isn't it?'

'It'll only be a couple of weeks.'

She didn't even have to think about it. 'Sorry, Scott, but I can't catch it. You know what it's like with my mum. If she falls again, I'll have to go round there and help Dad pick her up. I can't be in the slightest danger of giving her this bug. If you've even been inside a hospital, there's a big chance you've got it and—'

'It's okay.' Cullen smiled at Angela as she passed. 'I'll find somewhere else.'

'Don't be like that, Scott.'

'No, I shouldn't have asked. I didn't think.'

'Look, I'm being… Look, I know you meant well and I'm proud of you protecting Craig and Chantal, but you need to be just as protective of me and my family, okay?'

Cullen tried to swallow the thick lump in his throat. 'Okay.'

'You cook that chicken and do that gravy and we'll talk later. Okay?'

'Sounds good. I'll pick it up with my clothes and head—'

'Scott, I've really got to go. Lennox has caught another community death that might not be Covid-19 and has me leading it.'

'Sounds like fun.'

'It's never fun. I like you, Scott.'

'Like you, Evie.' With a smile, Cullen put the phone away.

Much as he hated it, Evie made him think of a sort-of ex with massive commitmentphobia, not that it got that far. She would put up all these barricades against him. And with good reason, but still.

It's not like they hadn't been an item for three years and been on four fortnight holidays in that time.

Still, she just needed time to make her decision. Not his; he had other options, but staying with her felt pretty good right now.

Cullen walked over to the entrance.

Angela was holding the door open for him. 'Mr Loverman...'

THE CUSTODIAL MANAGER'S office was even worse than Methven's office back in St Leonard's. Cramped and fusty with most of the space devoted to two walls of CCTV monitors showing every aspect of the prison's interior. Which didn't seem to be much. Usually, the place would be thrumming with energy at this time, with the lags heading back to their cells. All Cullen could see was a solitary guard walking down a corridor.

'Lockdown, eh?' Joe Dowling crunched back in his chair and bit into a bourbon biscuit, sending crumbs cascading down the front of his uniform, joining a splodge of what Cullen took to be hot chocolate. 'Been an absolute 'mare.' He smoothed down his thick moustache but didn't clear all of the crumbs. 'Poor Carlo had to step down to cover the shortfall.' He sighed. 'With what happened at the infirmary, I'll have to dust off my old truncheon, I tell you. Methven's your boss, aye?'

'For my sins.'

Dowling laughed. 'Well, he was saying Carlo might never smile straight again?' He slurped hot chocolate from his mug then dunked the biscuit in. 'I mean, not that he's much of a smiler, but getting panned in like that just for doing his job? I mean...'

And while one guard was on the way to Jimmy Deeley's lair in the Cowgate, another was getting his jaw rewired, Dowling was eating biscuits.

Cullen needed his help, though. 'That risk's all part and parcel of what we do, isn't it? One of my lads lost four front teeth breaking a door down.'

'Ouch.' Seemed to put Dowling off his biscuits for a few seconds. 'Your boss says there's a nationwide manhunt on for them?'

'That's the thing. As you should know, we've recovered Kenny Falconer and he's in custody awaiting transfer back here.' Cullen checked his notebook again, not for any reason other than to stop having to look at Dowling's ugly mug. And that boil looked ready to pop. 'Sir, the issue is that we still don't know the identity of the other prisoner.'

'And there's the thing, I don't either.'

'How?'

'Long story, mate.' Dowling pointed at the bank of screens. 'I've asked the lads to do an all-hands roll call, but there's a big protest about safety in here. The inmates aren't exactly happy about what's going on.'

'You mean the pandemic?'

'Right. They don't feel their health is being taken into account.' Dowling looked at Cullen, then Angela. 'I mean, between us three, the time to worry about that was before you stuck the nut on someone or defrauded someone's granny or whatever. But we'll protect them; that's our job.' He reached over for another biscuit. 'Long and short of it, Inspector, is we won't know who's missing until they decide to calm themselves down. I mean, I've every sympathy with their cause but I've got five lads unaccounted for just now.'

'Would any one of them be Kegsy?'

'Kegsy?'

'Kenny Falconer let the name slip. Might've bribed some of your lads.'

'*Bribed*?'

'Do you know of a Kegsy?'

Dowling bit into his biscuit and chewed for a few seconds. 'There's a lad goes by that, aye.'

'Can you find him on your magic screens here?'

'Right, fine, but I don't really need to.' Dowling picked up his phone and hit a button. 'Hiya, Dongle, see that Kegsy boy down your bit—' He nodded slowly, eyes locked on the biscuit plate. 'No, that's what I thought. Cheers, and I'm still due you a couple of pints so next time I see you... Aye, cheers, Dongle.' He carefully rested the phone down. 'Kegsy was in the hospital, being tested for Covid-19, but he was ailing and needed intensive care so Davie was moving him on to the Royal Infirmary. Needed to be put on a ventilator according to Dongle there. David Gilchrist, the guard supervising Kegsy, he was the one Kenneth Falconer stabbed.'

'What have you got for this Kegsy?'

'Let me see.' Dowling tapped at the keyboard. 'Here we go. I'll print it for you, pal.' The printer behind him whirred into life. 'Oh, would you look at that. The father is one of your lot. A DI Brian Bain.'

Cullen's blood froze. 'What did you say?'

'No middle name.'

'But you said Brian Bain?'

'Aye. The escapee is his son, Kieron Bain.'

14

BAIN

'Open wide!' Hard to tell the gender of the nurse. Or even the species, likes. They're dressed in a hazmat suit like we're in Chernobyl and I'm glowing green or something. 'Wider!'

'I'm fuckin' gaping here.' But it just comes out as a gargle.

They stick this six-inch swab into my nose and it's ten times worse than hay fever, goes down into my mouth and right to the back of my tonsils and it fuckin' hurts. Rummaging around in there like I'm the bad boy here. Like I'm carrying this fuckin' plague. Like a rat.

Fuck sake.

And the swizzle stick is back out and this lad or lassie sticks it in a wee bag. Like being in a custody suite. 'Okay, you're in luck. We've got a Cat Three testing facility just down the block. Your test will get processed this afternoon, so keep your cellphone on.'

I let out a breath. 'Thanks.'

'I suggest you stay in this quarantine area until we know for sure.'

'Right. Will do.'

And they leave us to it. Stuck in a plastic box, just me and my racing fuckin' thoughts and a smashed-in mobile.

Fuck, this must be what all those gays felt like back in the eighties. Not knowing, but suspecting...

And...

Fuck. I mean, this isn't as deadly as AIDS, but it's ballpark, right? And if you're unlucky enough to—

My fuckin' phone goes. Hard to make out who's ringing us through all the cracks. But it looks like it begins with an A, so it must be the little lady. So I answer it. 'Hey, did you call it in?'

'Yeah, I did. They said they'll look into it. Baby, I'm at your dad's place. He's not here.'

'Are you sure? Could be in the cludgy?'

'No, I'm inside. I've checked. He's not here.'

Fuck, fuck, fuck. All this shite with Art fuckin' Oscar and I'd forgotten all about my old boy. 'You said your mum was going round?'

'Aye, she's outside. Hasn't seen him.'

Shite, fuck, shite. 'Hold on a minute.' I kill the call and hit Dad's number.

Answered straight away. So he's not missing!

'Dad, you've scared the living shite out of—'

'Brian, it's me.' And it is her. Shite. 'He's left his mobile behind.'

Fuck sake. Halfway across the world and my fuckin' father's missing.

'My old man... He's... Where the fuck is he?'

She's breathing hard, like she's walking fast. 'I don't know, Brian. But I need to get home. Mum's there and—'

'Sure, sure. You get home. Okay?'

'Uh, yeah. What are you going to do?'

'No idea. I'll give you a bell when I know more.'

'Okay. Love you.'

'Love you too.' I kill the call and sit back on this lumpy, lumpy chair.

And everything hurts. My legs, my back, my buttocks. Both arse cheeks now. I mean, how the fuck do you injure your arse?

Fuck sake, this room feels like a prison.

When I'm back home, working like normal and bossing it,

anything goes wrong with the old boy and I'll be straight round there, sorting shite out like a fuckin' pro.

But I'm a long way away and there's fuck all I can do. The missus is toiling with everything we have to cope with and I'm being a selfish prick here.

Nah, fuck that. That's just the Onion Man talking. That snide little shite who gets at you when you've had too much booze, whispering all that hate in your ear when you're fuckin' fucked. Not exactly a session today, but it's sometimes worse when you sober up. I mean, I must've been just under the limit when we nicked that boy's motor.

And that head shrinker talked about the Onion Man and how to deal with him. Called it hangxiety, or something. Said to focus on what I can control, what I can do right now. Don't dwell on the past as I can't change that.

Load of horseshite, but I know how to play the boy at his own game.

Still has a fuckin' habit of biting us on the arse, though.

And fuck, it's still sore.

I check through my phone again and, through the cracks, I think I've got the numbers for all the hospitals Dad could've gone to. One in Livvy, three in Edinburgh. That's a fuckin' start, right?

So I dial St John's in Livvy. If anything's happened to him, he'll most likely be there. Right?

'We're sorry, but due to an unprecedented call volume, we are unable to take your call. Please call your local GP's surgery. If your matter is an emergency relating to the coronavirus, please attend in person.'

Beep.

Shite.

I hit redial. Fuckers usually put this up to deter timewasters.

'We're sorry, but due to an unprecedented call vol—'

'We're sorry, but—'

'We're sorry, but due to—'

Shite.

I need to find the old bastard. Where is he?

I've got to get home, back to Scotland. Back to sanity.

Should call the Home Office, get on the next flight back home, even if Elvis can't get on. Got to get back to find him. Save him.

He's missing *now*. And I'm stuck here *now*. But it's too late. Way too late. If we'd flown back from Florida, I'd be home and ready to crack skulls together.

No, I need to find someone to track down my old boy.

And there's only one man I can trust.

15

CULLEN

'Thought Kieron grew up in Dalkeith, though?'

Cullen glanced over at Angela. 'That's the thing. Like his old man, he never grew up.'

'Is that supposed to be funny?'

'It's true, isn't it?'

Angela shrugged.

'But as far as I remember it, Kieron lived with Bain and his wife in Bathgate. They divorced a few years back, then she moved to her parents' home in Dalkeith, which she inherited. I think. Kieron lived with her, became a cop. Trusted the wrong arsehole DS, stole some evidence for him, got busted for it. The rest is history.'

'I know. I was there, Scott.'

'Right. Hard to keep it all straight in my head these days.' Cullen felt all the years of service pressing down on his shoulders. 'After all the shite with Kieron went down, she sold up and bought this place.'

And what a place it was. The house occupied a double plot overlooking the golf course. Three-metre tall wooden fences with an expensive-looking entry system. Given what her son had done, Diane Cameron – formerly Diane Bain – clearly thought she needed protection. Or maybe it was just from her ex-husband.

Two cars in the parking bay outside. And in every other bay nearby. And it was the sort of neighbourhood where a strange car would draw attention. Besides, any sort of commotion could alert Kieron to the presence of cops. Assuming he was anywhere near.

So Cullen drove off through Emery's View, one of those quiet streets every developer was throwing up nowadays. Bigger plots, a good gap between neighbours, enough garage to fit three cars, and not directly overlooked. And they charged through the nose for them.

Last time he'd been in this exact stop, it was an old shale bing, a giant mound of earth kicked up in the sixties to extract oil to refine at nearby Grangemouth.

Cullen had walked this beat in uniform, and thought he knew the area inside out, but it had changed a lot. On the outskirts of Pumpherston, an old village now swallowed up by Livingston, but itself taking in new developments like this one. Close enough to the motorway but far enough away from the worst estates. And Cullen could rank them any way you wanted. Livingston was the archetypal Scottish new town, designed in the sixties to house emigres from the slum clearances in the bigger cities, and placed in specially chosen locations where they could grow and thrive. And Livvy was still growing.

But all that growth and capitalism meant that the first free parking bay Cullen could find was what felt like half a mile from the address. 'This'll have to do.' He pulled up and killed the engine.

Angela got out first and smoothed down her sleeve, the armband with new chevrons to signify her Acting position. 'So these stripes are basically Bain's?' Not that she had them yet. They only existed on a sheet of paper. Actually, they only existed as words on Methven's lips, not even an email.

'Something like that.' As they walked, Cullen tried calling again, but the call was either bounced or didn't make it across the Atlantic. That, or Bain had run out of data by downloading all that My Little Pony porn. He stabbed his finger against the redial button, wishing it was Bain's eyeball. And still the call failed. 'How long can he keep ghosting me?'

'You're not exactly top of his Christmas card list, are you?'

And just then, Cullen's phone rang. The Killers, *Mr Brightside*. Meaning one man. One stupid arsehole.

Cullen answered it. 'You decided to stop bouncing my calls, then?'

'Sundance, this isn't the fuckin' time for that shite. I need you—'

'You're right, but it's too late. I can't save you from this one. You buggered off to America for a fortnight *without formal approval*. And you signed off DC Gordon's holiday too.'

'Sundance, I'm sorry about that, but I need you—'

'No. Stop. I stood up for you when no one else would. I put my neck on the line for you with Methven and this is how you repay me? Not even so much as an apology?'

'Okay, okay. I'm sorry. Happy now?'

Not particularly. 'You used to constantly tell me off for my lack of professionalism.'

It still hurt. All the times he'd tried to save Bain from the mercies of Methven, and the stupid prick had let him down big time.

What's worse, he'd made him look like a complete idiot to Methven and his bosses, made it look like he couldn't control his team.

'Brian, I'm two men down now because of you. And you've been ghosting me.'

'Sundance, there's something up with my old man.'

'Your dad?'

'I'm not fuckin' talking about my husband, am I? Christ.'

Cullen didn't know his father was still alive, or that he'd had one, and would have put more money on Bain having a boyfriend. He had kind of assumed he'd been grown in a lab somewhere. And as much as he wanted to get on with it, he knew Bain wouldn't let go until he'd got his oar in first. 'What's happened?'

'I'm still stuck here, but I need you to head round there. The wife's not heard from him today and he's not answering his door. Called in on her way back from work and he's not in.'

Christ, this was rich. 'Look, I'm in the middle of something here, Brian, I can't just—'

'Sundance, I am *fuckin'* begging you here. Please. He's not a well man.'

'Look, I'll see what I can do. Text me his address.'

'Please. I need you to do it now.'

'After the way you've been acting?' Cullen sighed. 'I'll head there soon. Okay?'

'Thanks, Scott. I fuckin' mean it.'

'Tell me you're on your way back to Scotland.'

'Next flight. Swear.'

Cullen would believe that when he saw it. 'Listen, the reason I've been calling you is that Kieron's escaped from prison.'

The line went dead. Or at least it sounded like it. 'Fuckin' fuck's fuckin' sake.' More silence. 'Are you fuckin' winding me up here? This is not even remotely—'

'Wish I was winding you up. A guard was stabbed and killed, another severely beaten.'

'Fuck sake.'

'Kenny Falconer escaped with him.'

'What? He's hanging around with that wee shite?'

'We've recovered him, but we need to find Kieron. Anything you can do to help us bring him in will—'

'That fuckin' shite is dead to me. You hear?'

'I hear, but do you—'

'I've no idea where he is, Scott. Sorry.' And it sounded it. He'd not called him "Sundance" for the first time in what felt like years. 'And if I knew anything, I'd tell you. Just, please find my old man. If Kieron's on the lam, Christ. He might've taken him.'

'Why do you think that?'

'Well, they're close. Despite all the shite Kieron's done, the old boy's still kept in touch with him. Gets to speak to him on the blower, on account of his... mobility issues.'

Finally some sort of lead, then. 'Okay, text me his address.

Catch you later.' Cullen killed the call and his phone buzzed with a Livingston address. Not too far away. But this was a much more likely avenue. He set off again with renewed purpose. 'I swear, when Bain gets back from America, he'll be lucky to have a job.'

'It's Elvis I feel sorry for. He probably thinks their little trip is above board.'

'Hard to feel too much sympathy for him, though. Recording a podcast in America. What a pair of idiots.'

Angela glanced round at him. 'You know how much they're making from it?'

'What?'

'Elvis was telling me he's had to set up a limited company to make sure they don't get fleeced for tax.'

'Seriously?'

'I mean, I don't know what this pandemic will do to it, but he reckoned they were on track to make at least fifty grand this year. Each.'

Cullen felt like someone had punched him in the stomach. 'Just from talking about *beer*?'

'Craft beer, Scott. Lot of breweries throwing money at them. Makes you wonder why they still do the day job.'

Cullen could only shake his head as they walked up to the gates. He pressed the buzzer and tried peering through the gaps in the fence, but the panels of wood were offset to prevent such nosing.

'Hello?' A female voice, sounded local. Maybe Edinburgh. And definitely familiar.

'Police, ma'am. Looking to speak to Diane Cameron.'

'Can I take your name and warrant number?'

Cullen spotted a small camera lens hidden behind some darkened glass. He held his warrant card up to it. 'DI Scott Cullen.'

'Be out in a sec.' And it sounded like she said "Shabba".

Cullen frowned at Angela. 'Did you hear that too?'

'What, Mr Loverman, you thought she said Shabba?' She was grinning wide now. 'Guilty conscience, much?'

The gate opened automatically, with a smooth motion like

those fancy drawer closers Cullen used to mess about with in John Lewis when bored shitless during a shopping visit.

And Yvonne Flockhart stood there, hands on hips. Her long hair was in a loose ponytail and she didn't have the usual makeup on.

Evie.

Cullen's girlfriend.

What the hell was she doing here?

Cullen walked up to her. 'What's—' And it hit him. 'This is the unexplained death?'

'Sure is.' She got out her mobile and tapped out a message to someone. Typical. Then she put it away and craned her neck round him, but her eyebrow was arched at Angela. 'Oh, hey there. Been a while. Heard you're a sergeant now?'

'Christ, *I* barely know that. And it's only Acting.'

'Still.' Evie pursed her lips. 'Lot of that going on right now.' She grinned at Cullen. 'So that's three of you Edinburgh muppets all in Acting roles?'

Angela raised her eyebrows. 'I'm hardly a muppet.'

'No, but Scott and Crystal Methven are.'

Cullen rolled his eyes at her. Did she really think that? 'Listen, we're—'

Footsteps clicked across the dark stone path. DI Terry Lennox was striding towards them, hands stuffed in his pockets. Still junkie thin, but at least his hair was cut down to a sensible length these days. Made him look slightly more cop than dealer. 'Scotty Cullen.' He held out a hand, waiting for him to shake it.

'I'm not even going to fist bump you, Terry.'

'Smart. How the devil are you?'

'Adequate.'

'Adequate, eh?' Lennox laughed, way harder than was natural, then he put his hands back in his pockets. 'So. What brings you here, Scott?'

'Two Saughton prisoners escaped from the infirmary in Edinburgh. Kieron Bain was one of them.'

'Oh God.' Evie huffed out a sigh. 'The victim's son?'

'So it's a murder?'

'Not so fast.' Evie fixed him with a hard stare. 'Listen, Deeley's still working away inside. And I'd invite you in, but it's a crime scene.'

Lennox held up a finger. 'A *potential* crime scene. This could all just be a misunderstanding.'

'So is it, Terry?'

Lennox stared off into space for a few seconds, then looked up at Cullen. 'Let's go for a wee walk, DI to DI?'

'Sure.' Cullen followed him, giving Evie and Angela a shared nod, then strode across the limestone path leading around the house. 'So?'

'Heard you're back on the beat while all this is going on?'

'Right. Took a gang of reluctant homeless people into a hostel.'

'Beats this work.'

'You want to bring me up to speed?'

'Okay, so Diane Cameron called her GP a week ago on Monday, complaining about a sore throat and a fever. Been hell at St John's in Livvy and the ERI is getting battered too, so the doctor told her to self-isolate. Next thing we know, she's dead.'

Cullen saw into the living room now.

A pale woman lay slumped on a reclining chair, a duvet tucked up around her. Mouth open, staring up at the ceiling.

A figure in a crime scene suit was inspecting her. Jimmy Deeley, unless there was another pathologist with that exact curvature of belly.

'Paramedics showed up a couple of hours ago and recorded it as another Covid-19 home death.' Lennox sighed. 'So many of them out here. People are shit scared to go to hospital in case they catch the virus. Trouble is, a lot of them have got it, only they don't want to go in to hospital in case... Well. Going on a ventilator is no fun.'

'So why are you guys here?'

'Yesterday, we got a number of calls from her son, Kieron, from inside prison. Kid was desperate, saying it wasn't Covid-19. Said his mother was being held captive and insisted it was murder.'

'How does he know?'

'Search me.' Lennox stared over the tasteful pebbles and garden ornaments. 'That was my next port of call, but if he's on the lam? Shite on toast.'

'When was he told?'

'Yesterday morning. A guard by the name of Carl Kelleher broke the news to him.'

'Kelleher's in A&E himself. Broken jaw.'

'Ouch.' Lennox winced. 'The only good side is we've got a load of different numbers Kieron's been using, presumably borrowed mobiles from other inmates. The prison service can get them shut down by the networks.'

'You think there's anything in this?'

'Let's just see, shall we?' Lennox nodded inside the house.

Cullen looked in the house again.

No sign of Deeley now, just the victim. Bain's ex-wife, mother of his son. Dying like that didn't bear thinking about.

The front door clattered open and footsteps crunched across the gravel.

'Ah, Young Skywalker.' Deeley was tearing at the crime scene suit, his smile twisted by a frown. 'What brings you to sunny Livingston?'

'Kieron Bain's escaped prison.'

'Well, unless he's an expert at hide and seek, the boy's not in there.'

'Lennox here says he—'

'Aye, aye.' Deeley kicked off the trousers and tossed them into a discard pile. 'And you're wondering if there's anything in his fanciful theory this was a cover-up?'

'Go on.'

Deeley screwed up his face as he thought hard. 'Well, from what I gather, Ms Cameron presented Covid-19 symptoms, but hadn't been tested. Usual drill, told to stay at home and self-isolate. Then she turned up dead.'

'So did Covid-19 kill her?'

'That's the thing. I'll need to get some fast-tracking done, but it looks like she's been poisoned.'

16

BAIN

Fuck sake, this place is chaos.
When we left with Art, the hotel was empty. Now? Now, it's like the fall of Rome. There's a queue of irate punters trying to check out stretching right over to the fuckin' lifts. I mean, just fuckin' *go*! Get!

And the fuckin' arseholes are blocking the fuckin' lifts, meaning one thing...

STAIRS.

I open the door for Elvis and it's like four fuckin' flights. Won't just be Art Oscar's ticker packing in, I swear. 'After you.'

Elvis grips the handrail but doesn't start climbing. 'You know you can talk to me as much as you want, right?'

'I am.'

The boy frowns at us. 'Eh?'

'I am talking to you as much as I want here. Which is fuck all.' I barge past the wee shite and start up the stairs, two at a fuckin' time. I'll show these cunts who's boss!

'Bri!' Elvis is already out of breath. Fuckin' say what you like about cops of my vintage, at least we were fit, unlike this jobbie. Boy's a desk jockey, good for the occasional rummage on CCTV, but see if it's about him nailing some boy to the wall in a square go? Nae danger. 'Come on!'

Up to the first floor and, I tell you, this isn't so bad. Legs are feeling *gooooood* and my breathing's solid. Should defo get back to the running, I think.

'I think you need to talk to me. What's going on?'

'Elvis...' I stop at the landing between the floors and step aside.

This big red-faced good ol' boy comes down. Hawaiian shirt and suitcase you could hide a body in.

Elvis catches up with us. 'Come on, Bri. Talk.' He's looking at us with genuine concern in his eyes.

Christ, aside from her indoors and my old man, he's the one constant in my life. The one guy who'll stand by me. I act the cunt on that podcast, taking the piss out of him, but that show... It's my life. Might be just talking about beer, but we're talking about so much more. It's like that *Zen and the Art of Motorbike Maintenance*, it's all about the subtext. And Elvis makes it happen. Records it, buys most of the beer, edits it and uploads it. Fucked if I had to do all that shite myself. Well, I'm okay at buying the beer – most of the stuff I get it in is damn fine – but the rest of it? Fuck knows.

And he's been getting all the business side ship shape, too. Advertising piling in, likes. Breweries desperate to get a fuckin' toasting from the Billy Boy. And I tell you, right now, I much prefer being Billy to Brian fuckin' Bain. Almost fifty grand this year already.

'It's what you were saying, Elvis, about Sundance and Crystal Methven being after my head. It's getting to me, man. Last few years haven't been so good for me, have they? Used to be the golden boy. Jim Turnbull's best DI, great clearance rate, competent team. And now that's all in the toilet. Those two have it in for me.'

'That what you think? That Cullen's trying to get rid of you?'

'Don't dignify him by using his name. Sundance is fine.'

'That's not what I'm getting at. You think they're trying to get rid of you?'

'I do.' My nostrils are burning. Better not be coming down with that Covid shite, I tell you. 'Soon as we get back, just you watch. And this podcast's the only thing I've got that isn't shite.'

'What about—'

'Och, fine apart from the old home life. I mean professionally. We're doing a great thing, Elvis. Supposed to be talking to three hundred punters in that auditorium tonight. Three hundred to hear us two talk shite with Art Oscar. I mean... Thank you.'

'Cheers.' He can't look at us, though. 'But that's not what I mean. You've been weird since the hospital.'

'Had time in that room, didn't I?'

'Come on. Out with it.'

He deserves the truth, to be honest. So I step aside again for two Japanese boys in sharp-as-fuck suits to walk past, then set off up the stairs again. 'Truth is, I had to ask Cullen to look in on the old boy, right? Only thing is...' Fuck me, saying this shite out loud... 'You mind Kieron? My son?'

'Before my time, Bri. You don't talk about him.'

'Good reason for that, Elvis. Boy's dead to me.' Up past the second floor now, come on, still got this. 'Few years back now, the stupid prick was on the job. Uniform constable in Ravenscraig in West Lothian. Found a body in a Range Rover at the foot of a shale bing, but I think it was a bit more like he was there when the engine was started, if you catch my drift. Then he stole some evidence from a case to protect a mate of his.'

See talking about this? Fuck me, getting your balls battered by a bunch of wee neds has *nothing* on this shite, I tell you.

'Mate of mine, too. And Cullen's old boss.' How fuckin' times change. 'Kieron and him got involved with some stupid pricks and...'

Have to stop at the landing for a breather, likes.

More footsteps coming down. A well-to-do couple, her lugging all the bags, him shouting the odds at her until he spots us. 'Howdy.'

'Fuckin' mental this, eh?'

Boy frowns at us like I'm the mental one, and heads on past Elvis.

I let him catch up with us, recovering some of my puff.

'So, you were saying about Kieron?'

'Aye, I've not seen the wee toerag since he got sentenced.

Ten years, and this was seven years ago. Let's just say he's not exactly demonstrated much good behaviour inside.'

'Brian…'

'Cullen was saying Kieron's escaped from the jail.'

'What?'

'While we're going through hell over here, Cullen and the happy gang are out hunting for my son. Kieron and this wee fud who likes to stab people. Sold knives to half of Edinburgh's underworld too.'

Elvis is puffing hard now. So hard he stops on the next floor landing and grabs the door handle like he's clinging on to dear life with it.

'I mean, I believed Kieron. He said he was innocent. Paid a fortune to Campbell fuckin' McLintock to defend him, didn't I? I mean of all people. But it was all lies. Fucked my own career too as well.'

'What?'

'Went tonto on that fat bastard Jim Turnbull. Ended up the only option I had left open was going back to fuckin' Glasgow. But I don't like to be defeated, so I came back. And I still aim to take those cunts down a peg or three.'

'What are you talking about?'

'Cullen, Methven, Turnbull. They're all getting it in the fuckin' neck.'

'Bri, this is mental. You hate being a cop. You've got enough service to retire. This podcast, it's your future. People love you talking about beer with me.'

'I know you're just trying to sweeten me up, Elvis. Are those sex masks for you and me?'

'Stop talking about them! They're for Hallowe'en!'

Hold my hands up to the boy. He gets a ribbing, but he knows where to draw the line. Unlike me. 'Sorry, take it all back.'

'Seriously, you're the star of the show. I just edit it and top and tail your rants. People love the Billy Boy.'

'Aye, maybe.'

'We've done this whole *Escape from New York* lark, we're getting on that flight, okay?'

'Classic film, that. Fine. Come on, then.' I grab the handrail and jump up the next flight two at a time. Nobody's fuckin' stopping Brian fuckin' Bain!

But Elvis still downstairs points at the fuckin' massive number four on the door. 'Bri, this is our floor.'

'Bollocks.' Better down than up, though, so I dance down the stairs like that boy in the clicky heels. 'Thank fuck for the Yanks and their stupid numbering starting at the bottom!'

'Tell me about it.' Elvis leads along the corridor and sticks his keycard into the door. He gets the green light, and holds it open for us.

'You know, I take it all back about your cards. Mind that hotel in Portland where I took the piss because you lost yours?'

'And you kept yours in your wallet.'

'Aye. Take it all back.' I step into the room and stop dead.

Some cunts have raided the place.

It's a fuckin' bomb site, I tell you. Clothes everywhere, crushed empty beer cans, suitcases in the middle of the floor. Left my old laptop, but I don't blame them.

Suitcase.

Shiiiite!

I scuttle over to my bag and the fuckin' pocket is already open. And empty.

'This is a nightmare.' Elvis is grabbing at my arm like a wean. 'Let's just get out to JFK and get on the plane. Fuck this shit.'

'Sorry, Elvis, but that's impossible now.'

17

CULLEN

Cullen looked around the front garden, feeling like there was a gaping hole drilled into the pit of his gut.

He'd pinned their two escapees as the same type of psychopathic arsehole, the type who'd stab a guard to avoid their sentence.

And he'd been accurate in Kenny's case. He'll be serving at least one other life sentence after today's antics.

But Kieron...

He'd escaped because his mother had died, and he believed she'd been murdered. Or that she was gravely ill and not being taken care of. Either way, all that time inside – must be close to seven years since he was sentenced – must've rotted his brain, destroyed all semblance of logic.

But he wasn't here. Meaning he could be doing anything to whoever he believed had murdered his mother.

And Cullen needed to find him.

He looked back over to Deeley. 'You're sure it's poisoning?'

'Christ, Scott, I wish you'd listen to me.' Deeley was scowling at him. 'I said it *looks like* she's been poisoned. Be tomorrow before I can confirm at the post mortem.'

'Any chance you—'

'I mean...' Deeley shook his head. 'There was an ambulance

crew here. Number of deaths like this, the funeral homes and my lads... We just haven't got the capacity to shift them.'

Evie narrowed her eyes at him. 'Aren't you—'

Cullen shot a look at her, warning her to ease off. 'Why do you think she was poisoned?'

'Two distinct reasons.' Deeley stared back at the house. 'First, I've seen a *lot* of Covid deaths in the last week. Trust me, we're *nowhere* near the worst of it. My April is going to seem like absolute hell, and I thought my March was bad enough.' He picked up his medicine bag. 'And the clincher is – and I'll need to confirm this – there are corneal deposits of an unknown substance and the optical nerve appears to be inflamed.'

Which meant nothing to Cullen, but at least Deeley was on top of it. As much of a grumpy sod as he was, he was someone he knew he could trust. 'What do you think killed her?'

'Not so fast.' Deeley wagged his finger. 'Last time I gave any of you lot a clue before I'd done the maths, I ended up in court, didn't I?' He was glaring at Lennox. 'So, I'll leave you to figure out how to play it.' He shuffled off towards his Mercedes.

Lennox kept pace with him. 'Any chance you can—'

'Tomorrow morning. I'll invite both DI Cullen and yourself, Terry. You can decide who's attending. Okay?' A flash of lights and Deeley jumped into his car.

Cullen stared at Angela, then at Evie and then Lennox, standing next to her. Here they were, two sergeants and two inspectors. Shame that his half were only Acting, but hey ho. 'Okay, so how are we going to play this?'

'Well.' Lennox got out his phone and checked it for messages, then put it away again. 'The way I see it, Scott, you're looking for an escaped convict, who we urgently need to speak to, so we should team up. But we should also split up.' He nodded at Angela. 'DS Caldwell and I should speak to Kieron's cellmate and any known associates inside, see if he blabbed about who he thought killed his mother.'

'You think he's likely to have talked about it?'

'Maybe.'

'You think they're likely to share with you?'

'Worth a shot, isn't it?'

'Suppose.' Cullen sighed. 'So you're happy for me and Ev—*onne* to team up?'

'It's not like you're in a relationship, is it?' Lennox laughed. 'And you're professionals, aren't you?'

Cullen smiled. 'With my reputation?'

But, as much of a cowboy as Cullen was, he was trying to act like a pro. And he was constantly chasing the carrot of full tenure that Methven dangled in front of him.

And besides, the trail was leading precisely where Bain needed it to. After all, Bain senior going off the radar the same day his son escaped from prison...

That wasn't a coincidence, was it?

CULLEN CHECKED HIS PHONE AGAIN, then looked up at the address.

Pearce Court. A turn-of-the-millennium low-slung sheltered housing development, all white harled walls and faded wooden boards, long overdue a top-up of varnish.

Cullen killed the engine and opened his door. 'But you agree that this is too much of a co-inky-dink?'

'Aye, you think you're so funny.' Evie reached over and pinched his cheek. 'But aye, it's too much of a coincidence. You think Bain's jailbird son would really go after his dad?'

'Kieron's an ex-cop in prison. Who knows what that would do to someone. Then he gets told his mother's died of Covid-19 this morning. I mean, he's acted quickly, I'll give him that.'

'You lot were quick to believe his story.'

'It was more Lennox shutting him up.'

'Kieron didn't mention any suspects?'

'Not by name. Said he'd tell us once we'd checked it out. Lennox thought he was just playing us.'

'Great. So Kieron thought you weren't going to investigate and he—'

'Don't assume anything, Scott.' Evie stepped outside and slammed her door. 'And you're okay working this with me?'

'It's Angela I feel sorry for. Stuck with Lennox.' He grimaced. 'Bit strange how you haven't told him we're an item.'

'It's my private life, Scott.'

'And it's both of our professional lives.'

'Relax, Scott. It'll be just like old times. Except you're a DI and I'm still a DS. Besides, Lennox is a pussycat. Which is the problem.' She stared off towards the address. 'Number sixteen, aye?'

Cullen opened the front door and let her go first. Lack of security here was a bit of a concern. 'So Bain says.'

'That little creep.' Evie made her way along a dimly lit corridor, off-white walls marked at hand height, like the residents had to prop themselves up as they trudged along. She looked over her shoulder at him. 'You won't mind me leading in here, will you?'

'By all means.' But something wasn't right. Cullen sped up slightly to walk in step with her. 'Is everything okay?'

She stopped and took a deep breath. 'No, Scott, it's not okay. But we'll talk about it later.'

'This is about taking down Ken—'

'Later.' Evie turned another corner.

Part of Cullen felt like he couldn't win. But then, he had previous with risky antics. Risky antics that got people seriously injured. Or killed. He set off again, turned the corner and stopped dead.

Evie was outside a door, baton locked and pressed against her shoulder. A glance at him, then a step forward, with a finger to her lips.

Cullen found his baton and snapped it out.

The door was hanging open. Not enough that a neighbour would spot it at a distance, but resting against the door jamb. A quick 360 showed no other doors like that.

'Sure this is—'

Evie tapped her baton on a white piece of plastic to the side. *Dr J. Bain* was stencilled on it. She held up three fingers, then just her thumb, then her forefinger.

Cullen waited for her three count, then followed her inside.

'John?' Evie was taking it slowly. One step, then a look in all directions, then another step, another look. Rinse and repeat. 'Mr Bain, are you in here?'

Now Cullen was inside, his guts churned at the dual prospect of Kieron being there, and at Kieron attacking Evie.

But the room was empty.

Of people at least. Another bedsit, a single bedframe pressed against a wall, covered in a tartan bedspread, immaculately tucked in.

Not much of a kitchen, but high-end units and well put together. Just enough to store and zap ready meals. A worn armchair sat in front of a small TV, but both looked expensive, especially the antique TV cabinet which looked like it was worth more than Cullen's car. On the coffee table between them was a bottle of Dunpender single malt whisky and a smoky glass, one that looked constantly in use and was never cleaned.

So Bain's father was an alcoholic. That explained so much.

Cullen lowered his baton, felt his pulse slackening off. 'Well, there's no sign of him.'

Evie was scowling at the whisky. She didn't seem happy. 'Any ideas?'

'I've got one but I don't like it.'

18

BAIN

'THEY STOLE MY PASSPORT!'
Fuckin' break the golden rule of getting your way in a hotel, don't I? Shouting at the cunts, number one way to get fuckin' hee haw.

The boy behind the desk steps back from the barrage. 'Sir, I need you—'

'No. Listen to me, son. Back home, I'm a detective. Okay? I hunt down thieving wee shites for a living. Now, you let me get in there and have a decco at your CCTV and I'll get off and find my passport. Okay?'

Christ, have I triggered the boy or something? He's looking broken. 'Sir, I'll need to get approval from my manager.'

'No, you don't. This place is going to shite. Your boss will be using this as an excuse not to deal with anything. Just let me at it, then you can go back to dealing with this lot.' I wave at the queue snaking behind us.

The boy stares off into the middle distance for a few, then nods. 'Okay.'

'Just show me where, and I'll do the rest.'

'Over here.' He leads me to this big desk at the back and it's like those fancy Apple computers in John Lewis. He enters a password and steps away. 'There you go.' He walks back over to the desk and speaks to the next in the queue.

Here we go, time to show Elvis a thing or two about how to work this stuff. I take the mouse and move it.

The fuckin' cursor stays where it is.

Fuck sake!

Try the keyboard, but nothing.

'Here.' Elvis swoops in from nowhere and nudges us aside. 'There we go.'

The mouse pointer is moving freely now.

'How did you— Never mind.' I take over again.

This app thingy is not bad, have to say. Floors and corridors. Ours is just up on the third, by the lifts. Fuckin' tell you, never take a room by the lifts. Piss artists clattering in at three in the morning and whisper-shouting. The constant ding of the lift and "Third floor." Aye, darling, you've told us that fifty times tonight already. Fuck sake.

I take it back to twenty minutes after the wee incident with the gang and the ambulance and set it playing.

Elvis sits back on something. Fuck sake, the clown's brought his suitcase. He looks at us. 'What? I'm not leaving it like you're doing with yours.'

'All those sex masks still—'

'There.' He jabs a finger at the screen.

And lo and behold! The boy from the ambulance is there. Got my bum bag and takes out the wallet, then puts the keycard in the reader. Sneaky little look both ways then he slips inside.

Elvis is shaking his head. 'I told you in Phoenix you shouldn't keep your room number next to the keycard.'

'How the fuck am I supposed to remember it?'

'Stick it in your calendar on your phone like a normal person?'

'Got an answer for everything.'

On screen, the boy slips out. Just carrying my bum bag. I hit pause and stare at the cunt.

Elvis scowls. 'Why didn't he take my laptop?'

'Because it's an antique, just like its owner.'

'Cheeky sod.'

I hit the print icon and the wee laser to the side jumps into life. 'We need to find this boy.'

Elvis is transfixed by the screen. Talk about being triggered. All that time spent staring at CCTV and he can't pass a machine without losing half his soul to it. 'So what's the plan?'

'Find this cunt, kick his cunt in, then get the fuck out of Dodge.'

'And how do you plan to do that?'

'Got a solid idea, Elvis.' I score the paper and walk off. 'Come on.'

ELVIS IS SHAKING his head at us. 'I still think this is daft.'

We're out on the street again and don't fuckin' talk to me about Hell's fuckin' Kitchen... Art's motor is sitting there on the street. Filled with germs and that bug that's fucked everything up. 'Ach, it'll be fine.' I open the door, but maybe this isn't so smart. 'I mean, we can just take Art's car, find the gang who took my wallet and get my passport back. Bosh.'

'Aside from us getting into a plague wagon like that,' he flicks his hand at the motor, 'we have no idea where those boys are.'

I look down the long-as-fuck street, stretching way into Downtown or Uptown or wherever it is. 'Just up there, five blocks, we'll find where the ambulance was, and they'll be around somewhere.'

'Admit it. This is a stupid idea.'

'What's the alternative?'

He's glancing around all over the place. Can't look at us.

'Going to be two days getting a replacement passport. And we'll miss our flight. Unless we get the current one back, we're stumped. I've got to go to the embassy and fill out their forms, then sit tight until they magic up another one. In the middle of a complete disaster. Who knows if there's anyone even there? If it was most people, they'd have fucked off for the hills at the first cough. And the fuckin' embassy's down in Washington, DC, right? It'll be a consulate here or something. Will they be able to help me?'

Fuck sake. Those wee bastards, chorying masks from an

ambulance? Fills me with burning rage so bad I can feel it in my bones.

Someone's phone's ringing. Takes a few to realise it's mine.

Swear the cracks are even bigger now. Doubt the bastards will let us board a plane with it, too.

Can't see who's calling us, but I hit the answer button anyway.

And nothing.

Fuck sake!

So I press it again and something changes on the screen at least, so I put it to my ear.

'Brian, it's Scott.'

Takes another few to figure out who it is.

Looks like Elvis is going to get in the bloody motor. I mouth 'Sundance' to him and he nods.

'Brian, we're at your dad's place and—'

'You found him?'

'No.' Sundance does one of those sighs he fuckin' does all the time. Tell you, he's got marbles in his head or something. Doesn't exactly put me at peace, does it? 'Is it possible Kieron could've taken your father?'

'What?'

'There's no sign of your old man, and Kieron's escaped. You want help putting two and two together?'

And as if this couldn't get any fuckin' worse. 'Why the fuck would *he* kidnap my old boy?'

'There's something I haven't told you.' Another sigh down the line. 'Brian, Diane is dead.'

'What?'

'Your ex-wife, Kieron's moth—'

'I know who she fuckin' is! What's happened to her?'

Elvis is frowning at us now.

'Sorry, Brian. We think she's been poisoned.'

And it hits us like a fuckin' shovel in the gob. Followed by a clawhammer in the baws. Have to steady myself on the bonnet of this motor.

'She's dead?' I let out a deep breath. 'I hadn't heard.'

'Sorry to break it to you like this.'

'Ah fuck.' Hits us like a sledgehammer in the plums.

Fuck sake. All those times I've been on the other side of this coin and I thought the family of the victims acted fuckin' weird. Now it's me and I'm falling to fuckin' pieces here!

'Has Kieron killed her?'

'He's been calling Livingston MIT. He thinks someone has killed her. Didn't say who.'

'Have they done a post mortem?'

'Deeley's checking it tomorrow to confirm if she was poisoned.'

'In the name of the wee man...'

'Is it possible Kieron thinks your dad murdered her?'

Takes us a few seconds to unpick his words there. One thing about Sundance, his brain's a lot quicker than his mouth. 'Aye, Scott. It's possible Kieron thinks my old man killed my ex-wife. Diane used to see the old boy every couple of weeks. Poisoning's a fuckin' coward's game. And it's all my old man's capable of.'

'Do you have any idea where Kieron would go?'

'You expect me to know where that wee fuckbag would go?' Fuck sake. I've got to get home, got to sort this out. But I'm so fuckin' far from being able to do that. Only option here is to help that fanny Sundance catch my fuckin' son before he kills my old man!

'Is there anyone on Diane's side who—?'

'I lost touch with that side of the family when we divorced.'

'Did she remarry?'

'Aye, I think so. Maybe not remarried remarried, but there was a felly. No idea about his name or anything.'

'Okay. That's something we can look into.'

I feel some tears straining at my throat here. This has got the shite up my back, I tell you. 'Please, Sun— *Scott*, I'm begging you. Find Kieron for me.'

'I'm trying, but—'

'What's the warden saying?'

'The warden?'

'Christ, he lives in a sheltered housing place! Find the warden!'

'Okay. Thanks.' And he's gone.

I sit back on the bonnet of this motor and rub at my eyes. 'This just gets more and more fucked.'

Elvis still hasn't crossed the threshold of the motor. 'What was that?'

'I can't even...' And I can't. Voicing it is... *Christ*. 'Still no idea how to get my passport back. And I've got to get home because my scumbag son is going to murder my old man and this is all so fucked.'

Elvis smiles at us. 'You want to get a beer?'

'Do I fuck!'

As much as I could do with getting so fuckin' twatted that this whole thing turns out to be a dream, trying to deal with all this shite when the fuckin' Onion Man is whispering those sweet somethings of his into my ear? Fuck that.

'We need to get my passport back.' I put my phone in my pocket and touch something.

Wait a sec. I take it out and it's that cop's business card.

Charles Holten.

Sing ho-fuckin'-sanna!

19

CULLEN

Gordon Jackson looked as run down as the sheltered housing he managed, and not much older. He looked barely twenty, but had deep rings under his eyes like he'd never slept in his life. His shaved head was somehow sunburnt, though it was surely months too early for it to have come from the sun. But the rest of his face had escaped that fate so it was unlikely to be from a bed. Weird. He shook his head. 'I mean, that boy should be in a care home. This is for reasonably independent people.'

Cullen sat in a chair, almost knee to knee with Jackson and Evie. The cramped office somehow had a faint muddy smell, though he couldn't place it. Shelves on three walls, filled with various knick-knacks, including one devoted to those metal-faced plug-in kettles that'd burn your hand as soon as you switched it on. Presumably they were broken and awaiting fixing. 'You talk to anyone about putting him in a care home?'

'Well, I keep saying it to his son, but he's bloody useless. Doesn't listen to anything. And his *swearing*...'

Cullen could just imagine those words falling on deaf ears. Or being drowned by a whole shitload of F-bombs. 'What did he say about it?'

'I think he's in denial, to be honest.' Jackson looked out of the window in the direction of John Bain's tiny flat. 'They both are. I mean, part of the covenant of being here is that you're supposed to be able to look after yourself.'

'And Mr Bain can't?'

'Dr Bain. And no, he needs a mobility scooter to get around. Lucky he's in a ground-floor flat here, but I can't remember seeing him on the blessed thing.'

'What was he like when he arrived?'

'Better. It's been a slow decline. His son was looking after him, but he couldn't cope with it. He promised to look after him in here, get him fed and all that, but his heart's just not in it. Boy shows up every Sunday with a couple of boxes of the cheapest ready meals, some bread and a few bottles of whisky. I mean...'

'Anyone else visit?'

'Well, the son's partner. Can't remember the name. The...' Jackson frowned at Evie, then leaned in to Cullen. 'I don't know what the *PC* term is, but do you say Asian? Oriental? Whatever the right term is.'

'Okay.' Cullen thought back to the ribbing Bain had soaked up about his wife's Thai heritage. Still, this was the first person he'd met who'd actually seen her. 'What about his grandson, Kieron?'

Jackson frowned. 'He's the one who's *inside*, aye?'

'If by "inside" you mean prison, then yes. And I'm not aware of him having any other grandchildren.'

'Oh, he's got a wee girl, barely a year old.'

'Wait, what?'

Jackson was nodding. 'Kelya, I think her name is. Keeps talking about her.'

Jesus Christ. If that was true, Bain had been keeping the secret of having a *daughter* from Cullen. Who else knew?

And he couldn't be distracted by this. 'But John does talk to Kieron?'

'Son got him a mobile at Christmas and he's never off the thing. All those free minutes have been a lifesaver to him, but I'd hate to pay his phone bill once those are up.'

'So, I've got a case of a missing pensioner who is immobile, and a jailbird grandson. Any ideas?'

Jackson frowned for a few seconds, tapping his foot off the floor. 'There was someone here asking for him.'

'What did he look like?'

'Just a sec.' Jackson pulled out a heavy-duty laptop from a shelf. Looked brand-new, and pretty expensive. Green and blue lights flashed across the back as he jabbed a finger across the trackpad. 'Here you go.' He swivelled the machine round.

The screen was really bright, like staring into the sun, so Cullen reached over and turned it down a notch. The black-and-white footage showed the outside of the building, overlooking the car park. The time clock read just over an hour ago.

A mid-grey Fiat 500 pulled up and sat there for over a minute on quadruple speed, with the engine pluming in the cold late afternoon. Whoever it was, they were casing the place and taking their time doing it.

The sort of thing a cop would do.

The door jerked open and Cullen paused it. Hard to get a good view of the man, no matter how slowly he clicked through the individual frames, which seemed to be captured every three seconds, until the man was inside.

Cullen tried to overlay his memory of Keiron Bain, as a pimply young cop, but this man was much bulkier. Then again, a lot of free time in prison. Wouldn't be the first to build serious muscle in there.

'The lad wasn't here that long.' Jackson reached over, like he was annoyed someone else was using his pride and joy, and skipped it forward just over nine minutes.

The ground-floor door opened again and a man was wheeled out. Cullen paused to get a good look. He was an older version of DS Brian Bain, his beard longer, his hair a lot more straggly, but he had the same reptilian look about him. The same hostility to the rest of the world.

A few frames on and his companion walked out. Prison had aged Kieron badly. Cullen had last seen him when he was nineteen and now, seven and a half years later, he'd taken on his father's grey pallor, though he had escaped the baldness for now. He rushed over to the car and helped his grandfather in the back.

One final look and he got in the front. Seconds later, the grey Fiat whizzed off.

And they had the plates.

~

TURNED out the Fiat was baby blue. And was now on fire. Even at this distance, the flames still burnt at Cullen's skin, so he had to step away.

Still, they were lucky to find it. A back road to a back road that just so happened to have two number plate cameras either side of the entrance.

'Smart move.' Evie was standing by their open passenger door like she was using it to shield herself from the heat. 'The amount of product you pour on your hair every morning, you'll go up like a Roman candle if you get any closer.'

Cullen didn't quite believe her, but he didn't want to chance it, so he retreated to a safer distance. 'I'm not that bad, am I?'

'You're not that good, either.' She waved her phone in the air. 'The firies are on their way over.'

Cullen looked back at the flames, then at the woods surrounding them. The car was in a clearing and it was damp enough that the fire was unlikely to spread. And it didn't show many signs of it.

Why collect your grandfather in a stolen car only to torch it?

Was John Bain inside it?

Cullen kept tilting his head to the side, but all five seats looked empty. The boot was popped too, either left that way or forced open by the heat. And Cullen would have recognised the telltale bacon smell of burning human flesh and hair.

So Kieron had taken him, then dumped the car. Where to next? Was he doing this to make John Bain suffer even more?

But where? John Bain wasn't exactly mobile, even in that scooter. Had to be nearby, or he had to have got in another vehicle. Not that an escaped prisoner could easily get hold of one. And yet he had.

Cullen sat behind the wheel and slumped back. 'Have you spoken to the owner?'

Evie nodded. 'Nurse at ERI. Stolen from the car park outside.'

Cullen looked around again. It was getting dark. 'We're in the arse end of nowhere here. Where the hell has he gone?'

'Worth visiting that nurse?'

20

BAIN

This big fuck-off SUV slides in behind Art's plague-infested motor and Charles Holten gets out the driver side. Dressed in his civvies, wearing one of those coats with wee fuckin' tags on the shoulders and he looks even bigger than in uniform. He strides over to us and takes his specs off. Narrowed eyes scan me and Elvis. 'Guys, you need to listen to me. Forget about getting your passport back from them.'

I shake my head at the boy. 'Mate, I can't.'

'Seriously. Those guys are—'

'*Please.*'

He huffs out a sigh just like Sundance would. Two sighing brothers separated by an ocean. 'You should write it off. Get over to the consulate, plead and beg to get a passport today, then catch your flight home to England.'

Fuckin' England. 'Been on to them, pal. Say it's going to be two days minimum. The world's going to shite, so I doubt it's going to be that.'

'Yeah, so maybe you shouldn't have flown to Seattle and driven across this country.'

'How did you know about that?'

'One of the dudes in my precinct is a fan of your podcast.'

'Seriously?'

'Boyle's a big podcast guy, but yours is top of his list. Had tickets for your show too.' Holten frowns. 'Asked me to ask you what a "jing" was.'

'A jing? You're asking me about a—'

Elvis steps between us. 'Charlie boy, "jings" is an expression of surprise. And the whole thing is Brian's laboured pun on the Paul McCartney and Wings live album "Jings Across America". But it's nice to know our fanbase extends to the NYPD.'

Holten nods, but still doesn't smile. Cool as a fuckin' cucumber. 'Anyway, in my opinion, you shouldn't try and get it back. Your passport's gone.'

'Listen, pal. I fuckin' need it. My old man's in the shite back in Scotland and my jailbird son's on the fuckin' warpath and I need to get home and sort all this shite out. Please.'

He's looking at us, head tilted to the side. Looks like he might cave, actually.

'You know where they're based, don't you?'

Another Cullen sigh. 'Seriously. I'll drive you to the consulate now. It's not far.'

And right then, my mobile blasts out. And it's his brother in sighing. I hold up a finger and step away. My heart's fuckin' pounding here. 'Have you found him?'

'Sorry, no.'

'Fuckin' great. So I need to get over there and—'

'Kieron took him. And we've found the car, but it's burnt out.'

'Shite.' Fuckin' mallets smashing against my spine, I swear. 'Was my old man in it?'

'Hard to tell.' Can hear sirens in the background.

'Fuck.'

'Look, I'm not an expert and the fire brigade are just about here, but it looks like he wasn't in the car.'

'And that's supposed to be a relief, is it?'

'Brian, we really need to find Kieron. Anything you can—'

'Scott, I'm in the middle of hell here. Some wee toerag's stolen my passport and we're fuckin' stuck here. The consulate's fuckin' me over and...'

'Brian, we found the car just off the A801. A little back road that leads into the woods.'

'Near Bathgate?'
'Not far, aye. Go under the M8 and it's next right.'
'Shite.' Got it. Fuckin' got it! 'He's going for my wife!'
'Your Thai bride?'
And that professional demeanour slips to reveal the snide cunt underneath. Scott fuckin' Cullen, never a million miles away from making a stupid joke.
'Jesus, Scott. Really?' Some bird in the background giving him what fuckin' for.
Sundance sighs yet a-fuckin'-gain. 'Sorry, I didn't mean that.'
'Scott, that's just round the corner from my gaff. If he's got the old boy in his scooter, he could walk over there. Please, it might be nothing but can you go there?'
'Okay.'
I let out my own Sundance-sized sigh. 'Thanks. I'll text you the address.' I end the call and press the screen in hopefully the right places. Postcode, house number and loose description. "Big old place set behind walls." Fuckin' send.
And I'm still stuck here. Fuck sake!
Holten's frowning at Elvis. 'Why is he called Billy on the show when his name's Brian?'
'Now that, my friend, is a long story. The main reason is to hide the fact we're both cops, right. As for Billy. Well. You ever heard of William of Orange?'
'William of who?'
'Okay, then, we need to saddle up and—'
'Fuck this. I need to get that passport.'
They both look at me. 'What's happened?'
'Think the wee cunt is going for my wife.'
Holten looks at Elvis, and it's like something passes between them, some life force or whatever. Then he's looking back at me. 'Okay, buddy, we got you. Me and Paul here. We got your back.'
'So you're going to help me?'
'Not as a cop, but as much as I can as a human being.'
I hand him the CCTV print from the hotel. 'And your cop half knows where this gang's based, right?'

21

CULLEN

Evie pulled in across the road from the nurse's address and switched off the engine, but didn't look like she was in any hurry to get out. 'You think Kieron's here?'
'Maybe. He had to have a getaway from the hospital.'
'Okay, let's see what she knows.'
Cullen opened his door and put his right foot down. 'Aside from this being a murder, it's good working with you again.'
'It's very different, Scott. Just promise me you won't do anything stupid.'
Cullen raised his hands. 'I'm a changed man.'
She pursed her lips. 'Promise.'
'I won't do anything stupid.' Cullen got out and walked over. A paved drive led to an old stone cottage. He stopped dead.
"Bain House" was mounted into low stone walls, above open wrought iron gates.
'Seriously?' Cullen had to check the text again. 'Right number, right street. Didn't mention a name, though.' He sighed. 'Bain House? Really?'
'Hope this is just a co-inky-dink.' She stepped through the gate and crossed the long drive, wide lawns on either side. Baby blue garage door that would've matched the car's colour before it was torched. A large modern extension out the back, which

must've more than doubled the size of the house. Maybe even trebled it.

'Some place.'

Cullen rang the bell mounted on the middle of a posh-looking door, the same blue as the garage.

A shape appeared through the glass, walking towards them. The door opened to a crack and a woman frowned out at Cullen. 'Inspector?'

It took Cullen a couple of seconds to place her. Then it clicked. The nurse who had tested Cullen at the ERI. 'Apinya?'

'Right.' She smiled and, without being covered in PPE, her smile was infectious. 'What's this about?'

'I gather your car was stolen?'

'You've found it?'

'I'm afraid so.'

'Like that, is it?' She was holding a baby, hugging it tight, smoothing its back. 'Feeding time. Come in, then.' She turned and walked into the house.

Cullen gestured for Evie to go first, then followed her inside.

The place was beautiful and looked ready for a sale viewing. Off-white walls, with beige-painted panelling running halfway up, and a few elegant photos perfectly placed along the hallway. The engineered flooring didn't crack and grind with each footprint, unlike in Cullen's flat.

Apinya led them into a sitting room, with two lime-green sofas at right angles opposite a wall-mounted TV above an ancient fireplace. A fancy soundbar sat on top, playing some whale sound stuff. She held up the baby, gripping under its arms. 'This is Kelya, my daughter.'

Evie frowned at the kid. 'She's hella cute.'

'Thanks.'

'So about the car, where—'

'Look, I meant to call back in. I couldn't find the spare key the other day. Had to take my husband's.' Apinya frowned. 'You do know who I am, right?'

That sign outside wasn't a coincidence. 'You're Mrs Bain?'

'I didn't take his name, but yes, Brian Bain is my husband.

I'm Apinya Saelim. In Thailand, we didn't have surnames until like the twentieth century, so it's kind of a thing to keep them.'

'I see.' Cullen perched on the edge of a settee, but felt his eyebrows shoot up. 'I didn't know you had a daughter.'

'That's Brian for you.'

'He doesn't talk much about his home life.'

'And with good reason.' Apinya smiled again, but her look quickly darkened. 'He told me you were spreading a rumour that he bought me from a mail order catalogue and that I may have male genitalia?'

Cullen raised his hands, palms outwards. 'Sorry, no.' He caught a glare from Evie, then let out a sigh. 'Okay. Look, I was just winding him up.' He was blushing, could feel it in his cheeks. 'You need to understand what it's like—'

'Scott, I'm fully aware of Brian's shortcomings. He gets under people's skin. But his heart's in the right place. And I see a side of him nobody else does.' She cast her gaze to Evie then back to Cullen, then smiled again. 'And I know all about you, Scott.'

'From Brian's perspective.'

'Maybe, but he's a good judge of character.'

Not really what Cullen would say about him. 'Look, I'm sorry about that stuff. It's insensitive and I—'

'It's fine. But I don't think you know the real Brian. He's a sweet, kind man.'

'Feel like I'm in the wrong house here.'

'I'm serious. I know what you're thinking, though. When we first met, I thought he was a boorish pig. My friend Danielle brought me on one of those double dates that aren't double dates. Her and her boyfriend, Paul, and he brought along Brian.'

'Wait, Paul Gordon?'

'Elvis, as you call him.' She rolled her eyes. 'But yeah, Danielle worked in my parents' restaurant with me. Both waitresses and we stayed in touch when we went to uni. That first night, Brian was full of "eff" this and calling everyone nicknames, but I called him out on that nonsense. Got through to the real Brian Bain. And we fell in love.' She picked up Kelya and bounced her on her knees. 'I didn't think I could have kids, but two missed periods and this wee thing just showed up...'

'Congratulations.'

'It's a nightmare.' Apinya laughed. 'Both of us work full-time, so I have to rely on my parents a bit too much, you know?' She looked into his eyes. 'Brian went off the reservation by going to America, right? That's why you're here? Brian and Paul are trying to get their podcast off the ground. They've started making good money from it. Hopefully I can go part-time soon. Maybe pay off a big chunk of this mortgage too.'

'You know he didn't get that time off approved, right?'

Apinya looked up at the ceiling. 'I didn't, no.'

'Listen, the reason we're here is your car was spotted outside John Bain's home and—'

'Brian's father...' She pecked Kelya on the forehead. 'I swear, dealing with John is like having another child. This used to be his house. Seven generations of Bains have lived here. Brian and I bought it off him after his mum died. John wasn't coping and we tried to help him, but he needed supervision. Trouble is, John is a Bain. He's stubborn as they come.'

'I know all about that.'

'But my car was outside his house?'

Cullen sat forward on the chair. 'We're here because Kieron escaped from prison.'

'Oh my God.'

'And Brian's worried that you'd be a target, but it seems like Kieron's taken Brian's father. Could Kieron have got your car key from him?'

Apinya shook her head. 'Maybe. I've been taking Kelya to see John most days while Brian's away. Brian usually goes, but I think it's important to keep it up.'

'Does John ever talk about Kieron?'

'Brian won't let him. Just shuts him up about it. I've tried getting him to open up about it, but it's too raw for him.'

'Did John talk to you about Kieron.'

She bit her lip. 'Yesterday, John said he spoke to... to his grandson. And he was worried about his mother.'

'He say why?'

'Not really. Has something happened to her?'

Cullen glanced at Evie and gave her the slightest nod.

Evie cleared her throat. 'I'm afraid that Kieron's mother is dead. We've just had it confirmed that the death was probably a murder, most likely poisoning.'

'God. Now I think about it, John did mention something.' Apinya ran a hand down her face. 'According to John, Kieron was going on about his stepfather, the man his mother lived with after she left Brian.'

∼

EVIE SAT in the passenger seat, arms folded. 'C-O-R-D-E-L-L. And Stephen with a PH.'

'With you now.' Keyboard sounds in the background. 'Got results in West Lothian, Edinburgh, Fife and Midlothian. Want me to check Greater Glasgow?'

Evie shut her eyes. 'No. How many are you talking?'

'Forty-odd.'

'Great. Can you check for any previous addresses in Bathgate and Livingston?'

'Not really.'

'Okay, just email me the whole list. Thanks.' Evie ended the call and dumped her phone on the dashboard. 'Well, isn't that just grand?'

'Isn't it just?' Cullen looked back at Bain's house and had this horrible feeling that he could reach out and grab Cordell, but he was nowhere near. 'Any way we can narrow it down?'

Evie locked eyes with him. 'Not without a *ton* of shoe leather. Our Stephen Cordell could be someone who isn't even on that list.'

'I know. So close, but so far.'

'You okay, Scott?'

'Not really.' Cullen felt the itching in his scalp. 'What was it Churchill said about Russia? A riddle, wrapped in a mystery, inside an enigma? Even more applicable to Brian Bain. I can't believe he didn't tell me he had a daughter.'

'You guys have worked together for a while, aye?'

'Since 2011. You remember that case in a gym me and Craig did?'

'Vaguely. I remember what happened that night more.' Cullen blushed.

'Oh, don't be so bashful, Mr Loverman. Took us a while, but we found each other, didn't we?'

'Right. Sure.'

'Anyway, for nine years, he's been a Bain in the arse?'

Cullen winced. 'Don't give up the day job.'

'Come on, that's funny.'

'Maybe, but I'm not in the mood. You think she let Kieron take her car?'

'Maybe. Maybe not. But I've got an idea.' Evie thumbed her phone screen again, then a ringing tone blasted out through the speakers. The display read *Calling Lenny…*

'Lennox…' A sigh rattled the speakers, so loud that Cullen had to reach over to turn the volume down. 'What's up, Yvonne?'

'Have you spoken to his cellmate yet?'

'Yup, and two other inmates so far. Nothing.'

'Has anyone mentioned a Stephen Cordell?'

Lennox paused. 'Who's he when he's at home?'

'The stepfather. Kieron might blame him for murdering his mother.'

'Well, as you know, he didn't name any names on the many, many calls we received. And I doubt anyone in here will talk, even if he did blab to them.'

'Okay.' But Cullen was running out of options here. 'Anything from Deeley yet?'

'Oh, yeah, I got a missed call. He's left a voicemail. Back in a sec.' The line muted, then started beeping.

Cullen looked over. 'How do you cope working for this clown?'

'Drink.'

'Okay…' Lennox was back. Sounded like he was outside somewhere and near a building site. 'Just listened to Deeley's voicemail. Boy, he can rabbit on, can't he? Hold on a sec.'

The line paused again.

Then a blast of static. Sounded like someone was driving. 'Terry, I swear, if you do that again...' Deeley.

'Jimmy, you're on with Scott and Yvonne.'

'Right. And let me guess, you didn't bother listening to my voicemail?'

'Better to get it from the horse's mouth.'

Deeley laughed. 'Okay, long and short of it is we've run the blood toxicology and it appears that she's been poisoned with chloroquine phosphate.'

Cullen locked eyes with Evie. 'The main ingredient of those anti-5G pills Keith Ross was selling.'

'Who the hell is Keith Ross?'

'Never mind.' Cullen gritted his teeth. 'Terry, is Angela Caldwell still with you?'

'She's inside, but aye.'

'Ask her about the pills. Okay. Keep your phone on. Thanks, Jimmy.' Cullen got out his own phone and called Lauren Reid.

The dashboard sound changed from Lennox's mouth breathing to a windier sound. 'Sir, I'm kind of busy now?'

'First, don't call me sir. And second, this is important. You're on with Yvonne Flockhart.'

'Hey, Lauren.'

'Yeah, Yvonne. So what's up?'

Cullen leaned forward, like that would make any difference. 'Look, I need you to speak to Keith Ross again and find out if he sold any of those pills to a Stephen Cordell.'

'I mean, I would. Only, his lawyer's just turned up and wants to unwind everything the idiot's told us.'

A perfect day just got even worse.

'What has he told you?'

'Well, he's been naming all and sundry. People who've bought the pills off him, his supplier. That USB thing tipped him over the edge. He remortgaged to buy them.'

'But he's not mentioned a Stephen Cordell?'

'No, but hang on. Charlie Kidd's looking at his laptop.' Sounded like Lauren was running along a corridor. Background muffled chat, including a harsh "fuck sake". 'You're on with Charlie.'

'Right, Scotty?' Charlie's Dundonian drone filled the line. Didn't sound happy to speak to Cullen, but then he never did.

'What am I looking for?'

'The name Stephen Cordell.'

Hard keyboard tapping filled the line. 'Okay. Got an email receipt for one of those anti-5G dongles. Some shonky PayPal clone.'

'Can you tell if Keith sent the package?'

'Not that clear. Hang on.' More typing. 'Oh, just found the email trail. Looks like he hand-delivered it.'

'You got an address?'

22

BAIN

I mean, fuck sake. We'd have been *fucked* without this boy. Would be looking for those pricks on the wrong side of the river. And now we know which one's the right one.

Holten's driving us over Brooklyn Bridge. It's a fuckton less impressive in person than on the telly. You can't see fuck all because the daft bastards have put girders where the view should be. Fine if you're walking over, I suppose, but all I can see is the East River foaming below us and a big shiny building that's almost invisible against the sky. Fuckin' useless.

'Is that the Statue of Liberty?' Elvis is in the back, nose pressed up against the glass like a wee kid.

'Sure is.' Holten thumbs over his shoulder. 'You see those towers?' He grins. 'That's Downtown.'

'Right. Sure.'

We're coming in to land at the far side and it's like getting the train into fuckin' Newcastle. Unreal. Thousands of miles away and it's the fuckin' same as home.

Old wharf buildings are still hanging around among these bigger, newer ones. Least Brooklyn doesn't have the towers of Manhattan. Well, not that I can see through these big metal strut things.

The drivers absolutely hammer it over here, I swear. No danger you'd get up to eighty within ten miles of Newcastle city centre. Holten's barrelling into the right lane, the one to come off by the looks of it. Off-ramp, they call it, don't they? And it looks like we're coming off into central Glasgow.

Forget Geordieland, I swear there's fuckin' Sauchiehall Street up there!

Sure enough, Holten weaves us through some pretty thin traffic onto a ramp curving round to the right.

There's a boy on a motorbike up ahead with the stars and stripes on his leather jacket and Holten's up his arse, then he shoots off left as the road splits. Looks like we're not heading for the Expressway. I-278 according to the sign.

And all of a sudden we're out into an urban landscape. Big wide avenues with towers up ahead and loads of trees on either side.

Holten pulls a cheeky one and sneaks through a red light, then parks behind an ice cream van that looks abandoned.

One of those iconic buildings up ahead, curved brick windows and that. Probably call them lofts or brownstones or Christ knows what.

'Okay.' Holten kills the engine and eases off his shades again. 'The mayor's started a huge-ass crackdown on gangs raiding PPE from ambulances, so I know a shitload about them. And those guys you chased? They're in there.'

Across the road, there's this big fuck-off tower. Concrete and brick thing with six windows to a floor, with an air-conditioning unit sitting below each one. Can't even see the top from over here.

'Those dudes? They're a sort of anti-Wall Street thing. Not quite Antifa, but not far off.'

Give him a nod. 'So they're squatting?'

'Whatever that means.'

'Means they're...' Fuck it, no time. I hand the CCTV print again. 'Who is this boy?'

'Dude calls himself Elrond.'

Elvis pops his head between us. 'Like the elf boy in *Lord of the Rings*?'

'That's the one.'

'They armed?'

'Would I let you go within five miles if I thought they were?' Holten laughs. 'Not guns, no. But watch out for knives.' He looks over at me. 'I can't go in, you understand that, right? But I'll wait here for you.'

'No offer of a throwaway gun?'

'Just get in and out. I'm not here.'

Not that I know how to shoot one. 'Just tell us the floor and I'll crack the boy's skull.'

'Third floor. And the power's been cut, so the elevator won't work. One set of stairs. And please, don't crack any skulls.'

~

ELVIS POINTS out of the window. 'That can't be the Empire State Building over there, can it?'

'Focus!' I grab the door handle and my heart's fuckin' pounding in my chest. 'And it's the wrong fuckin' part of the city for it, you cretin. Need to be on that other bridge to see it.'

Am I really going to do this? Raid a bunch of Antifa bams to get back my passport?

Fuck it, it's not like I've got a choice here.

'Come on.' I ease the door open and step through.

It's like party central up here. All the apartment doors are hanging open. While Holten thinks they've shut off the power to the lifts, these boys have got some juice going into the flats. Like that fancy hi-fi I've got, the music is playing from all the rooms at the same time. And it's fuckin' pish. All deep booms and thin hi-hats going ten to the fuckin' dozen. What happened to music? When did it get shite?

Place reeks of dope like a student halls of residence. So they're all pretty cool, sitting around and chatting, nodding to some beat in the music that I can't for the life of me figure out.

Big pair of dudes are hanging out by the nearest doorway, hands in pockets. Could be brothers. 'Yo?'

I nod at the guy. 'Looking for Elrond.' Best John Wayne accent again, so there's no ambiguity here.

'What you want to speak to him about?'

Acting all sussed here, as they'd say on the streets. 'Got some info for him.'

'You five-oh?'

'I'm forty-five. Do I look that old?'

'I mean are you a cop. Five-oh, man.'

'Am I a cop?' I laugh and slap the big bastard's chest. Fuck, it's like a wall of granite. 'Hell no. Don't you know who I am?'

'Sorry.'

'Name's Billy. Of the Crafty Butcher podcast.'

'Podcast. Right.'

'And I'm passing on some info *about* the cops.' I sniff, giving us a wee break. 'And maybe get some... material from him.'

Dude frowns at us. 'Material?'

'Protective equipment. Masks, goggles, gloves.'

'Huh.'

'Got some big cash to spend.'

His pal thumbs behind us. 'Fourth door.'

Too fuckin' easy this.

'Cheers, bud.'

Elvis waltzes past. 'Thankyouverymuch.' Just like his namesake.

Clown.

I mosey on down the hallway like I own the place and knock on the door. 'What was that about?'

'Better than your John Wayne, Bri.'

This pretty lassie is sitting cross-legged on the floor outside the door. Her mate passes her a cigar that stinks of hash. Both aren't too impressed with us. Fuck, maybe we do look like cops.

'Call that a blunt, right?'

She holds it out. 'You want?'

'Not strong enough for me, darling.'

'Eh, bullshit?'

I squat down next to her. 'You know where I can score some crack?'

'Not here.'

'Shame.' I winch myself back up and get a stab of pain from my earlier escapades.

The door opens to a crack and a boy peers out. 'Come in.' Disappears but doesn't open the door, does he?

So I nudge it and walk inside.

Just three of the cunts sitting on a settee, same pinks and purples as earlier, playing some PlayStation football game on a giant telly. One's holding a joint between his lips, but his hands are on the controller and he looks like he's the one in charge of the boy with the ball, that Ronaldo lad. He chips the keeper and the crowd go bananas inside the virtual stadium. He passes the joint to his buddy.

And it's fuckin' Elrond, isn't it? Sitting at the far end, locked in concentration. His nose is all red and purple and definitely shouldn't be at that angle. Fuckin' got to take pride in my work, eh? He doesn't look up, just festers at the fact he's conceded another goal to his mate.

'You recognise me?'

He glances over, shrugs, then he's back at the game. The whistle blows and Messi's kicking off. Fuck knows what teams are playing here. 'Should I?'

'We met this afternoon.'

'Met a lot of people.'

'You've got something of mine.'

'Like fuck I do. Don't even know you, old man.'

Snide wee shite is locked into his game, sucking on his doobie hands-free. Treating us with fuckin' disdain.

Fuck this for a game of soldiers.

I shoot forward in front of the telly. The two pricks look up. 'Man, get out of the way!'

I grab the left one's left ear and the right one's right ear and slam their skulls together. Crack!

Fuckin' lovely!

Elrond chucks the controller at us and it catches my eyebrow and fuckin' hurts. He tries to get away, tumbling over the side of the sofa, and he runs through a door.

'Stay here, Elvis.' So I fuckin' follow him.

The boy's in the cludgy, sitting on top of the pan and cowering. 'What do you want?'

'You little shite.' I step in to the bog. 'Took my fuckin' passport, didn't you? Now you fuckin' *deny* it?'

'Man, you want to get back to England so bad?'

Fuck is wrong with these people. 'What part of fuckin' England do you think I'm from?'

'The area full of assholes?'

'Fuck me. Give me my passport. Now.'

'I sold it!'

'Don't fuckin' lie to me.'

'I swear.'

'Bullsh—'

The little shite slashes the air with a knife. The blade catches my coat and cuts through the material, scratching the skin.

Not in the mood for this shite, so I grab the boy's wrist and squeeze really hard, bend it downward while I trap his elbow against my side and mash his mug against the cistern. Just like that old cop up in Dundee told us. Boy knew a thing or twenty about pain and pressure points.

Got this little shite squealing. He drops the knife onto the floor tiles. I reach down to grab it, then press it against his throat. 'You've picked with the wrong cunt to mess with here, sunshine. I want my wallet and my passport. Now.'

'Okay, okay, okay!'

I let him up. 'You fuck me about, and I'll slit your fuckin' throat. Okay?'

'Sorry!' He points at the cistern. 'There. The fanny pack's there.'

I lift the lid and – lo and fuckin' behold – my bum bag! And it's dry as a bone. Wee sketch inside and the wallet and passport are both there. I'm going home! 'You're fuckin' lucky they're here, otherwise I'd be chucking you out of the window.'

'You going to let me go now?'

I invert the knife so he can take the handle.

He's looking at it, rubbing his wrist like his hand's fallen off. I mean, it's probably broken, the way it's hanging there. Then he reaches out for the blade.

And I stick the nut on him again.

He crumples back against the bog and tumbles over against the wall, and goes down like a sack of shite. I get a fuckin' good boot to his balls, enough to make sure there won't be an Elrond Jr any time soon, and smash his bonce off the wall, hard enough to dent the plaster.

'You don't steal from fuckin' ambulances!'

23

CULLEN

'Feel so bloody stupid.' Cullen kicked down a gear and shot past the parked fire engines, still battling the earlier blaze. 'Just down the road from where we found the car.'

'Yeah, but we didn't know about Stephen Cordell, did we?' Evie was gripping the oh-shit handle, eyes locked on the road ahead. 'Left here.'

'Okay.' Cullen pulled off the main road, hitting a rally drift to shoot off down a wide country lane. No road markings in the middle and barely wide enough for two cars.

Evie checked her phone. 'Half a mile on the right.'

'So Kieron's walked here? With his grandfather in a mobility scooter?'

Cullen's phone rang. *Lauren calling...* He hit answer. 'You getting anywhere?'

'Just been in with Keith Ross again. His lawyer understands the situation now and is helping us, shall we say. Keith's just confirmed that he did sell some of those pills to Cordell.'

'So much for social distancing.' Evie smiled. 'Okay, thanks Lauren.'

'Don't mention it. Just tell Scott not to do anything rash.'

'Story of my life.' Grinning, Evie reached over to end the call. 'Well?'

Cullen pulled up just beyond the address. Three cottages set back from the road, the parking bays in front filled with work vans. He tried to think it all through, but things were sticking inside his head. It was all just gunged up. 'Let me get this straight. Stephen Cordell killed Diane Cameron by poisoning her with Keith Ross's anti-5G pills?'

'That's about the size of it.' Evie frowned. 'How did Kieron know?'

'Not sure. Maybe he just guessed. Thought he'd stabbed her or something?'

'Maybe.' She raised her eyebrows. 'Scott, you know how we say "like you" on calls and stuff...'

'Evie, this feels like in a film when someone gets close to someone else just before they die.'

She rolled her eyes. 'I just want to know if it's more than "like".'

'It's a lot more than like.' He leaned over to kiss her. 'I love you.'

'Steady!' She pushed away like she'd been electrocuted, then got out of the car.

Christ...

Cullen got out into the stiff wind and a truck trundled past, honking its horn in a blare of passing sound. Not much of a warning, was it? He checked the three cottages. 'Which one is it?'

Evie pointed behind them. 'Through there.'

A pair of imposing gateposts, three times the size of those outside Bain House. Tall stone walls, cemented in place, and covered with moss. A long row of beech trees sat above it, crawling halfway over the road.

'Where the hell is back-up?' Evie set off through the gates, holding her baton.

Cullen followed, snapping his out. Never knew who was lurking around any corner. 'We should wait here.'

'Scott, no. We need to recce this place. Find out what we're dealing with.'

'And you say I'm the cowboy?' He passed through the beech into a clearing.

An old farmhouse with a circular drive outside, a mature weeping willow almost in the centre. A BMW SUV sat underneath the leaves.

No signs of life inside the house, but there was someone in the back of the car.

'Stay here.' Cullen set off across the pebbles towards the car, low and quick. He rounded the SUV's boot and popped his head above the window, then down again.

Took all that time to process who was in there.

John Bain, sucking on a whisky bottle like a baby from formula. A Dunpender, too, drinking a special-edition single malt like it was supermarket own-brand blended.

'Check on back-up, would you?' Cullen opened the door and got in. The car reeked of booze. 'Sir, I'm a police officer. DI Scott Cullen.'

'Very pleased for you. Your mother must be so proud of you.' John's voice had the same flat snarl as his son's, but it was a lot more erudite and educated, that particular brand of Scottish that didn't know much about housing estates and certainly wouldn't set foot in one. He took a swig from the bottle. 'Get out of here if you know what's good for you!'

'John, Brian sent me to help you. Your son?'

'That useless banana? He can take a running jump.'

Cullen wrestled the bottle out of John's hand, but it was like trying to separate a junkie from his needle. 'Where is Kieron?'

John couldn't take his eyes off the bottle. 'Not telling you.'

'He's inside the house, right? Is he after Stephen Cordell?'

John reached out a hand, clawing desperately. 'Give!'

'No. Answers, now.'

'You know who I am? I'm Dr John Bain. I was professor of mathematics at Glasgow and Edinburgh universities. Not at the same time. And you think you can play games with me?'

'Tell me what Kieron is up to, and I'll give you this bottle back.'

John stared at it with the micro-focus of the hardcore alcoholic. 'Wee Kieron's going to look after me, he says. We're going on our holidays after this. Place up near Lairg.'

In the Highlands. Cullen held the bottle closer, but not too close. 'Is he alone in there?'

'Well, he will be after he kills the man who murdered his mother.'

'What has he told you?'

'That man's a monster. Killed his mother! I'll tell you! Give me it!'

Not exactly the best idea, but what else could he do? Cullen didn't want John Bain screaming like a toddler for his whisky while Kieron was inside with Cordell, so he let him have the bottle. 'Okay, John, I need you to stay here, okay? And go easy on that stuff.'

'What, or it'll rot my brain?' John laughed. 'Wish it would, I'll have you know. The rest of me is an absolute disgrace, but the old grey matter is still golden. And I can't do anything with it except think and worry and fret and...'

Cullen checked John was still belted in and got out.

Evie was over by the front door, baton primed and ready.

Cullen joined her. 'We should wait.'

'What did he say?'

'Like father, like son, really.'

'Is Kieron in there?'

'Supposedly.'

'Going for Cordell?'

'Sounds like it. Planning to take him up to the Highlands too.' Cullen looked back at the main road. Another lorry hurtled past. Still no sounds of approaching police cars. 'We should wait.'

'You might be a cowboy, Scott, but you love it when I go cowgirl.'

Cullen tightened his grip on his baton, but it felt sweaty to his touch. 'Now's not the time for a joke.'

'Look, you're the ranking officer here. Hopefully Cordell's still alive. We can save him.'

Cullen nudged the door open and peered through into a large hallway. Would've been grand at some point, but now it seemed dusty and dark, and stuck in the sixties, the last time it appeared to have been renovated. He stepped inside and listened hard.

'You killed my mother!'

Okay, so that was definitely Kieron. Sounded like it came from straight ahead.

Cullen looked back, just as a squad car pulled up outside. 'Get them to secure John, then we're going in.'

'Okay.' Evie spoke into her radio, so quiet Cullen couldn't make anything out. 'Let's do this, then.'

Cullen waited for the pair of uniforms to get through the drive. A male and female officer, batons drawn. He jabbed a finger at the car, then set off through the door, locking his baton in place, then stopped outside the open door.

A kitchen, filled with battered old Shaker cupboard doors. An Aga sat in the middle and Kieron was pressing a man's face towards the hob. Cordell, presumably.

'PLEASE! NO!'

Cullen stepped forward. 'Stop!'

Kieron swung round, pulling Cordell upright and pressing a kitchen knife against his throat. Seemed to take him a few seconds to recognise Cullen. 'You? You fuckin' ruined my life!'

'Kieron, just let him go, okay?'

'Him? Fuck off. No way!'

'Kieron, it's okay. We can talk about this down at the station.'

'Aye? Last time I did that, you fucked me over. I'm doing fifteen fuckin' years because of that. Because of you.'

'Kieron, this isn't the place for this chat. And you don't want to make this any worse for yourself. At the moment, any jury would go very leniently on your escape attempt. It's completely understandable. But if you add in a murder? Forget it.'

'Why am I doing this then? Eh?'

'You think he killed your mother, don't you? And nobody listened to you.'

But it didn't seem to make any difference. 'Fuckin' hell, man, don't try that shite on! It won't work!'

'Kieron, it's okay.' Cullen inched closer to the cooker. 'Let's just calm down a bit here, okay?'

'Calm? You try being calm when you're stuck inside and this fuckin' *cunt* kills your mother! What can you do then, eh? EH?'

Another step forward. 'That's not for you to decide, Kieron.'

Cordell's eyes were bulging. 'Son, I was just trying to help her.'

Kieron pressed the knife that bit closer. 'How was killing her fuckin' helping?'

'Your mum had the coronavirus, son. The doctor wouldn't help and she was getting really bad. I was trying to cure her. Bought these pills from a lad on a group on Schoolbook. I saw all this stuff about how the virus is 5G and—'

'Those pills? Christ. I've been taking them.' Kieron tightened his grip around Cordell's throat. 'You been taking them too?'

'Aye, and I'm not well. Son, I didn't know they'd do that. They're supposed to stop it, protect us.'

'You killed my mother over a fuckin' *mistake*?'

'Please, son. I didn't know!'

'He's right, Kieron.' Cullen was only inches away now. 'Those pills are toxic.' He was close to losing this, though. 'We've got the man who made them in custody.'

'What?'

'He's going to be in prison too.'

But Kieron had the look of someone with nothing to lose.

'Kieron, we've got your grandfather in protective custody.'

Kieron looked round at him, frowning. 'What?'

'There's a squad of uniforms out there, Kieron. You're not getting away.'

Cullen stepped forward. 'Firearms are heading here too. And, as an ex-cop, you know what that means.'

Tears flowed down his cheeks. 'You don't know what it's been like. The shite I've been through in there.'

'Tell us, Kieron. It's fine.'

'Fuck sake, I was nineteen and I made a *mistake*.'

'Just let him go and you can see your grandfather.'

'Fuck sake, I'm not the criminal here. Dad isn't looking after him, is he? He's drinking himself to death in that flat.'

'I don't disagree.' Cullen got Kieron to lock eyes with him.
'What's your plan, Kieron? You going to the Highlands?'
'Right. I know a place. Well, Kenny knew it. His mum's dad's old home. I want to look after Granda. He's got money to look after both of us.'
'Kenny, your grandfather's not a well man. He needs professional care. Now, if you just let him go, then we can—'
'Fuck this.' Kieron grabbed Cordell's wrist and pressed his hand against the hotplate.

The room was filled with screams and the smell of bacon.

Cullen lashed out with his baton but Kieron parried the blow with the knife. He pushed Cordell into Cullen and they went down in a heap, Cordell landing on him and squeezing the air out of his lungs.

Kieron picked up the knife and pressed the blade against Cordell's throat.

A swipe of metal cut through the air and sent Kieron flying backwards, arms windmilling. Then Cullen couldn't see the rest, just heard a thud and another loud scream.

'Evie!' Cullen wriggled and pushed Cordell's prone body off him.

'Jesus!' Evie pulled Kieron away from the Aga. 'It was an accident.'

Kieron's left cheek was burnt black.

24

BAIN

We're gliding across that freeway we saw earlier, up so high it's like we're floating over Brooklyn. I look over at Holten. 'Say what you like about this country, you fucking know what you're doing when it comes to roads here.'

'It's pretty sweet, huh?'

'Telling you, we got from Portland to San Jose in like six hours or something. That's like driving from Aberdeen to Birmingham.'

Boy's frowning at us like he's got so many questions in his head. And it hits me.

'I don't mean the Aberdeen in Washington and the Birmingham in Alabama. Scotland to the Midlands. In England. And the roads are shite most of the way.'

'Drove in England once. Wouldn't do it again.' Holten eases off into the lane for another slip-road heading for the Long Island Expressway. 'You sure you don't want to talk about what happened back there?'

'Damn sure. And damn sure you don't want to hear it. Put it this way, Elrond won't be chorying any more masks.'

'Chorying?'

'Stealing. Christ.'

'You killed him?'

'Christ no, but he'll—'

Then my blower goes again.

I brush some more of the splintered glass away and it's fuckin' Sundance calling us. I put it to my ear. 'Yellow?'

'You're in a good mood.'

'I'm fine, Sundance. Just fine.'

'Must be. You're not calling me Scott again.'

'Only do that when you've been naughty, which is most of the time.'

He pauses, but it's not the time or place for kicking me in the balls. 'Your dad's safe and well. If a bit drunk.'

Fuckin' old bastard. 'See where I get it from?'

'He was really a maths professor?'

'Aye. What about Kieron?'

'Your son's in custody. He'll do another ten years for what he's been up to today.'

I look out the window at the city passing by. 'I don't have a son.'

'Brian, Kieron was taking revenge against his stepfather, Stephen Cordell. He thought he'd murdered your ex-wife.'

'And did he?'

'By accident. She was sick. He was giving her meds that turned out to be lethal.'

Fuckwit. 'Okay. What about Apinya?'

'She's safe too, Brian. And I'm sorry for all the shite I've given you about it. She's lovely, not that it's any defence if she wasn't.'

'I better go.' So I hang up and watch the skyline in the rearview. All those Manhattan skyscrapers, feels like a million miles away now. Like it's not real, like this is a dream.

But it's all fuckin' real. Too real.

Fuckin' Kieron.

I've made a lot of mistakes in my time, but that boy's the biggest one. Letting him grow up in a toxic environment like that... Not being there for him when we divorced, not supporting him when it all went to shite. Disowning him.

And I didn't even know his mother was dead.

'You okay?'

I look over at Holten. 'Fine and dandy.'

'You don't look it.'

I give him a shrug.

'Is Elrond still alive?'

'He's still breathing, aye. Might only be raiding ambulances with one hand and his baws are now located in his lungs, but he's alive.'

He fixes me with a hard stare. 'Just so we're clear, you're not coming back into this country again. You hear?'

'We've got to come back for our rearranged live shows in—'

'I'm not messing around here, Brian. You're fucking crazy, man, and I'll help you get out of the country, but you can never come back. Elrond will lodge a report.'

'Well, someone may have to help him with the big words, and hold the biro for him. Sure you can't make it disappear?'

'Not my precinct. And even if it was, I can't just lose paperwork. Don't know what kind of shitshow you guys run back in Scotland, but I've got enough of a bad name.'

'I fuckin' thrive off my bad name.'

'I'm serious.'

'So am I.'

'Listen to me. Quit it with the bullshit. He had your passport and wallet with all that ID. If he remembers your name and files a report, there'll be a federal arrest warrant for a man matching your description. You can't come back to New York if that happens. Probably the whole country.'

'Why are you doing this?'

'Aside from my family in Scotland, those were some bad dudes you took down. It feels like an away win.'

'You a football man?'

He's nodding. 'Soccer, sure.'

'Who's your team?'

'New York City.'

'I mean, British.'

'Oh. Uh, London Arsenal.'

'London Arsenal? It's just Arsenal...' Fuck it, let the boy have it.

Another sign for that expressway whizzes past and Holten gets into the right lane.

Kieron. Fuck sake.

I was *sure* he was going to take down the old man, sure he was going after the little lady. I had it arse about tit. Wrong fuckin' way round.

But he was a fuckin' vigilante. Christ knows how many extra years on his sentence, just to punish the fucker who'd killed his mother.

A lot of water passed under that bridge, I swear, but she didn't deserve to die like that. In her own home, poisoned by a fuckwit.

Kieron...

I look over at Holten. 'Can we go back to that hospital?'

'What? In Hell's Kitchen? Where you were tested?'

'Aye, but I've got to get something back from Art Oscar.'

'What?'

'Gave him a bottle opener. Wouldn't mind getting it back. It's got sentimental value.'

'This about your son?'

'Something like that.'

Holten narrows his eyes, but he's not shifting out of the lane for straight ahead. 'Just after my shift ended, I visited him and he seems to be recovering.'

'That's a relief. Mind if we—'

'It was a heart attack, not Covid. He's going to make a good recovery, thanks to you two.'

'Thanks to you and all, but if we could—'

'You could've just left him, and gone home. But you didn't. That's why I'm helping you. You're good people.' Holten reaches into his pocket for his house keys. 'He gave me a little thank you, but I guess it's what you're looking for, huh?'

I take his keys and it's there. A bottle opener with "Dad" stencilled in. I ease it off the keyring and run my nails against the indentation. 'Tell you, this thing has such a nice action.'

'Here's the thing, though. I'll keep an eye out and I promise to let you know if a warrant actually does get issued. Chances are a wannabe gangster ain't going to run to the cops because he got tuned up by a Brit.'

'Aye, prick thought I was *English*. Should've done both of his hands.' I grin at the boy, though. 'Cheers, man.'

25

CULLEN

Cullen knocked on the office door and waited. Felt like it took a long time. Way too long. So he hit the door again.

'Come!'

Cullen entered and nudged the door shut behind him. 'Sir.'

'Ah, Scott.' Methven was glugging from a can of Wakey-Wakey energy drink. Never a good sign. 'Have a seat.'

Cullen stayed standing. 'Your text was somewhat cryptic.'

'Sorry, but the walls have ears.' Methven gestured at the chair in front of his desk. 'Please, I insist.'

Cullen sat this time. These chairs were impossible to get comfortable in. 'Kieron's in the hospital.'

'Ah.' Another sip, frowning. 'How bad were his burns?'

'Sounded and smelled a lot worse than it was.'

'And is DS Flockhart okay?'

'She'll be fine. Made of tough stuff.'

'Very true. Well, you'll need to get a second Covid-19 test.'

Cullen rubbed at his throat. 'Already done.'

'Excellent.' Methven swung round in his office chair and reached over to the small inkjet printer on the table behind him. He took a couple of sheets, but focused on them instead of swinging back round. 'Okay, well, given that DS Bain will be arriving back in Britain tomorrow, I think it's important that we put our plan into action.'

'So you're going through with firing him?'

'Would you blame me?' Methven swivelled round and pushed the sheets across his desk. 'Most leave was cancelled, Scott. DS Bain was prohibited from going to the US, and yet he went. I believe his exact words were, "I'm not letting the fuckin' flu stand in the way of my big chance".' Methven's impression was flawless. 'Now, as much as I wish you were there to witness it, it was just my word against his.' He licked his lips. 'Until now.' He nodded at the pages.

Cullen picked them up. Three of them. The first looked like screenshots of text messages.

Methven: *Need I remind you that you are a policeman? You have a duty and this country is entering its direst emergency in seventy years if not centuries.*

Bain: *Blah blah blah. I'm in Portland and my direst emergency is my next pint. Take your job and ram it.*

Cullen slid it back. 'That's not good, is it?'

'No, and I have an exchange of emails between DS Bain and DS Gordon, vis-à-vis: *Elvis, your leave is still authorised. Don't listen to Sundance or Crystal. We're leaving for the States, man!* There were six exclamation marks in that one sentence alone.'

'Sir, I don't know what to say. That's enough to fire him, but I think we should consider a middle ground here.'

'Go on?'

'You can argue dismissal all you like, but I think we should consider demoting him to constable.'

'Why?'

'He's got hidden depths and skills.'

Methven peered over the edge of his can. 'Does he have anything on you?'

'Not that I know of.'

'Scott, the correct answer is that there's no kompromat.'

'I shouldn't promise that there isn't any.'

Methven shook his head, but he was smiling. 'If there's something I should know?'

'I'm joking. Well, aside from the fact DI Lennox doesn't know that myself and DS Flockhart are romantically involved.'

Methven snorted. 'And you paired up, didn't you?'

'It made sense. Look, with what's going on with Bain's son and his father, not to mention having a baby daughter—'

'What?'

'He didn't tell you either?'

'Nope.'

'He didn't even take paternity leave?'

'Well, no. I would've found out.'

'Right, well.'

Methven smoothed down his wild eyebrows. And failed miserably. They still stuck up like a pair of caterpillars. 'First, you'll be pleased to know that DS Caldwell's Acting position is now official. Paperwork has been signed and delivered. I expect you to help her through the sergeant exams ASAP.'

'Will do. Still doesn't give me an answer as to what we should do about Bain.'

'Look, Scott, I don't think this should be a matter for me to decide. You're an Acting DI, so you need to demonstrate that you're at the requisite level.'

And there it was, another carrot. Cullen actually missed Bain's stick-first approach.

'So I've got to throw another officer under the bus to *maybe* get my promotion made permanent?'

'That's not how I run things.' Methven reached into his drawer. 'But it can't be my decision, as I'm no longer DS Bain's people manager on the system, what with my DCI tenure now permanent.' The humble-bragging wanker pulled out an envelope and set it on the desk. 'You are.'

'But I'm only an Acting DI, sir. I'm a sergeant, technically the same grade as him.'

Methven paused, long enough to get Cullen's gut flurrying. 'So far, you've secured the arrest of, and obtained, a confession from one Kenny Falconer. He's going down for murdering a prison guard. Next, you've got a confession from Keith Ross on a mass poisoning that will likely solve multiple manslaughters, including... well. And you've brought in a fugitive. That's impressive work by anyone's standards. Carolyn Soutar and Jim Turnbull are impressed.' He slid the document over the table. 'Congratulations, Detective Inspector.'

~

CULLEN SAT in the ward's waiting area, staring up at the ductwork on the ceiling. Similar to what you'd find in most modern police stations. Why did new buildings not have ceilings? Why was it okay to just put pipes through the place like that?

Still, here he was, waiting for test results. He put a hand up to his forehead and he was sure he had a fever. And his lungs felt like they'd been crushed by a lorry.

He rocked forward on his chair and opened the envelope again. He had to check the document just to make sure he wasn't dreaming. But there it was, full tenure as a DI. And a *serious* bump in his salary.

'Scott?'

Cullen looked over at the male nurse beckoning him over. He put the envelope away in his jacket and got up to follow him.

The nurse – Clive, according to his name tag – was sitting in a sterile room behind a pale-white desk. 'So, the test results performed by my colleague this morning came back.'

Cullen took a chair, but could barely breathe. 'And?'

'They were negative.'

Cullen exhaled slowly. 'Thank God for that.'

'The state of testing in this country is appalling. We can't waste tests on police officers who decide to wrestle idiots to the ground. Nurses and other frontline workers need those tests more urgently. I've lost two colleagues to it already.' The nurse raised his eyebrows. 'So to have to perform two tests in the same day on the same officer?'

Cullen still gagged just thinking about sticking the swab deep in his mouth. 'And that's negative too, right?'

~

CULLEN WALKED DOWN THE CORRIDOR, rubbing his throat. Felt like he needed to clear his throat, but each cough just left something in there.

Evie was sitting in the waiting area, frowning. 'You okay?'

'No.' Cullen kept a good distance from her. 'I've caught it.'

'You're sure?'

'One negative test this afternoon, then a positive now.' He frowned. 'Have you—'

'Positive.' She got up and walked over. 'Technical term is pre-symptomatic, apparently.'

'How the hell could we have caught it from them? We weren't in close proximity for that long, were we?'

'Long enough. Plus the stress of the situation must've expelled more viral load. Maybe.' She smiled. 'The good news is that it's most likely to be a really bad flu for us. Right?'

'As long as you don't just mean a cold but *flu* flu. Influenza. It can be really bad. And if this is even worse? It'll be no picnic, that's for sure.'

'We'll get through it together, Scott. You can stay at mine. I wasn't very understanding when you called me about it earlier. It's just... After what happened with Craig and my last relationship, and then you and Sharon, I just didn't want to *have* to move in together until we knew this was it. But all I've thought about is you not having anywhere to stay. And I want to protect you, Scott. So if we self-isolate together, then maybe it can be a trial run?'

'That sounds perfect.' And it did. Right down in the pit of his stomach. He got out the piece of paper. 'Some good news, for once. And... I've got a really tough decision to make.'

EPILOGUE
BAIN

The next day

Fuck me, these proper respirator masks are a fuckin' ballache. Just will not sit comfy, will it?

And there's no sign of Elvis. Trying to get his fuckin' steps in, isn't he, so he's walking around the terminal. Doesn't matter that he's slap bang in the epicentre of a viral pandemic, does it? Ten thousand steps. Every fuckin' city we were in, exact same thing.

'Just need to get my steps in, Bri.'

Fuckin' roasting in Phoenix. Lucky he didn't get pulled up for it by some local cop.

I finish my IPA and leave my last five dollars as a tip. Woof ya, that was pretty strong. My legs are like jelly, but fuck it.

I've got my passport, my bottle opener and we're heading home.

I walk off down the corridor and I swear that same bookshop is every three units. Same one. Same books. Same selection of hoodies and none of them fuckin' fit.

And there's a door marked for dogs. I mean, are they pissing and shitting in there? Dog litter? I mean...

Fuck, there's our gate and Elvis is there, tapping his watch. Can't see the time on my knackered phone, can I? And I can't be arsed hurrying. Not that I can with these jelly legs.
'What's up, Paul?'
'Bit of an issue.' Elvis looks over at the flight desk. Not much of a queue getting on. 'The lassie says we've both got fevers so she won't let us on.'
'Ah, for fuck's sake.' That's it. I fuckin' storm over there and lock eyes with her.
Nice-looking lassie but frosty with it. Blonde hair that looks expensive. Could do with smiling, mind. 'Sir, as your friend says, I'm afraid that I can't let either of you board.'
'Listen, we were tested yesterday morning. Mount Sinai in Hell's Kitchen.'
'And have you got the results?'
'I just need to get back to Scotland.'
She clicks her tongue a few times. 'Sir—'
'Look, the hospital must have them.'
'Have you got a contact for the doctor?'
I frown. 'It's a Dr Santiago, I think.'
'You think?'
'Sorry.'
'Sir, I suggest you get in touch with your healthcare provider.'
'Sure thing.' I get out my phone and it's more like a fuckin' smashed-up watch than state-of-the-art technology. 'Let me see.' I hit dial and stand there. Never shift when you're at the head of the queue. Or line as they'd say over here. I mean, what's wrong with—
'Welcome to the Mount Sinai customer care line. We're sorry, but due to high call volumes we are unable to take your call.'
And it just dies.
Fuck sake.
I'm stuck here. And I need to get home.
I look at Elvis. 'You got your results?'
He's looking at his phone, then at me with a grin. 'Negative.'
'So it's just me stuck here? Fuck sake.'

'Bri, we can—'

'Hold on a minute here. You got an email?'

'Aye, why? Haven't—'

There's a fuckin' email there! That doctor, the one in the hazmat suit. Swear this country's health system is mental. The email's like it's come from my bank:

Mr Bain,

I write to you to confirm the results of the test for Novel Coronavirus (COVID-19), which you undertook at our facility on the morning of Friday March 20th, 2020.

I confirm that the test is **Negative**.

Additionally, I can confirm that our test is certified best-in-class and that international travel is allowed with the usual safeguards as recommended by your airline.

Finally, the symptoms you exhibited appear to be a result of fatigue to the point of exhaustion and excessive consumption of alcohol. Please seek medical advice upon your return.

Regards,
Dr Rosa Santiago, MD.

Cheeky cow.

I hand the moby over to the attendant. 'Here you go, sweetheart. Safe to travel.'

And fuck me hard and fast. The rest of the world is dying of this fuckin' bug and I've got a hangover.

BAIN'S KITCHEN

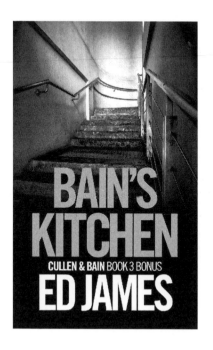

Author's Note:

This was a free bonus short story for people who joined my Readers' Club, included here for you. If you want to join too, then sign up at https://geni.us/EJmailer

Thanks and I hope you enjoy this!

SATURDAY
21ST MARCH 2020

BAIN

Fuck me but those lights are blinding. I reach up to switch them off, but my head's still nipping. But we're actually on the ground. It's daylight. Can't believe I slept through that landing.

Back in Scotland.

Man, how I have missed the place.

Across the aisle, Elvis is yawning and stretching out. Blinking hard, too. His dark stubble's almost swallowed up his sidies. 'You slept well, then.'

'Like a wean. Screaming and wetting myself.'

Two rows behind us, a couple are the only ones together, everyone else is spread out. Barely anyone aboard and I doubt many of them were daft enough to travel into the fuckin' epicentre of a pandemic. That's my cross to bear, I suppose.

A beep and the light comes on. And the rest of the punters get up and start rummaging in their bins over their heads.

I unfasten my belt but there's no point getting up. My suitcase is still in that fuckin' hotel, a fortnight's worth of dirty grundies and sweaty T-shirts and, fuck me, my socks. My feet are fuckin' rancid just now. Need to get that looked at again.

The boy behind gives us a nod. He's got that look I tried for a bit, shaved head and beard. Didn't work. Every fuckin' week, it took me ages to figure out where to draw the line, that tapering of beard into sidies. And it kept getting closer to the jaw, and just looked daft. So I'm like a wean in another sense now, smooth as fuck all over.'

Elvis waves his phone at us. 'Dani's just texted, Bri. Her and Apinya are waiting for us.'

And for the first time in a fuckin' fortnight, I feel that lightness in my soul.

∼

'Supposed to be here by now.' Christ, I miss her. 'And we're looking for a people carrier, aye?' Another check and it's all just cars. Not anywhere near as many as usual, mind, but still just cars.

'One of those Ford ones, like we had in Texas.'

'An Anal Adventurer or whatever.' Stuff my hands in my pockets to give us something to do. 'So where the hell are they?'

'Dani just said to wait in the usual place, Bri.' Elvis is sitting on his case. Thing is bigger than a fridge and, of course, it was the first thing off the fuckin' plane, but the stupid bastard thought it wasn't his. I mean... 'God, I've missed that wind.'

'Me and all.' And I have. Something particular about the cold Scottish wind that you don't get anywhere. Maybe the west coast of Ireland or Cornwall or somewhere, but it's probably too warm there. Cold, but not chilling. Refreshing maybe, despite us being at a fuckin' international airport with all those fumes and that.

But Elvis isn't listening, back to texting someone. Frowning, meaning something nice and juicy.

'What's that?'

He looks at us, but he's got that "in two minds" thing going on. 'Just got a text from Craig Hunter. Cullen is a full DI now.'

'FUCK SAKE.'

I mean of all the sneaky wee shites that walked the fuckin' Earth, it just—

'There they are.' Elvis nods off to the side, then kicks his case up and starts wheeling it over.

Fuckin' sight for very, very sore eyes. Aching ones. Might've slept on that plane, but I barely got a wink in America. I mean, that whole jetlag thing's supposed to be coming this way, but I never adjusted to the time over there so I can list the Starbucks that open at five in any city you want. Well, any that we stopped at on "Jings Over America", anyway.

Elvis slides the door open and is wrapped up by arms. 'Hey, Ellie. Missed you.'

'Here!' The driver's this big red-faced bastard who looks like he's about to have a stroke, and he's shaking his fist at us. 'Gonna get in, pal? Need to get out of here before my ticket's up!'

'Aye, sure.' Elvis laughs at something Danielle says that I don't catch. Boy's definitely punching above his weight with her, even though she's the size of a house now with that wean in her belly.

I help Elvis get his case in the back, and my own belly's full of tiny butterflies flapping their wings. Elvis flips over my seat and I get in next to Apinya.

And I feel complete.

She's sitting there, smiling, that intense look in her eyes, full of love and wisdom and knowledge. She hands me Kelya and I can't...

Just...

I let out a deep breath. A pulse of rage flashes in my skull, picturing Sundance as a permanent boss. But another look at Apinya and it's gone again. 'I've missed you. Both of you.'

'We've missed you too.'

'Here, son, you getting in or what? My ticket!'

'Calm your beans, mate.' Elvis slams the door and slumps back in his chair. 'That's us good to go.'

'Finally.' The boy pulls off and races through the car park.

We stop and I pass Kelya back to Apinya. 'You okay?'

'I've just about coped. Mum's been golden.'

'She's a saint, that woman. See where you get it from.'

'Hush now.'

'I mean it. I was lost before you.'

Outside, the boy's fannying about with the ticket machine.

Fuck me, it looks like he's going to have that stroke right now and one of us four is going to have to drive us home.

'Being away, it's...' I've got that lump in my throat. 'The only thing keeping me going is doing the right thing. Always try to do that as a cop, but those pri— em, people... won't let me win and they'll kick me off the force soon enough. My pension's fine, but I'm trying to get a new stream of income. That podcast is the one good thing I've got.' I lean over and kiss her. 'Except you.'

She chuckles and rolls her eyes, but I can tell she's feeling it too. Christ, being with this woman, it's like being on ecstasy. And being apart from her, I go back to being my old self. The fuckin' dickhead.

The door slams and the boy gets in the front. 'Right, that's that, then.' He takes a slug from a bottle of WakeyWakey – when did they start doing it in bottles? – and pulls off. 'That's us, folks. Next stop, Bathgate.'

I lean forward. 'Need you to make a detour on the way, mate.'

∽

THE OLD BOY'S just lying there, still breathing, still clinging on. His death would be a blessed relief, I tell you. Not just for me. He's fuckin' miserable. His eyelids flicker and his bleary eyes focus on me. 'That you, Billy?'

'No, Dad, it's Brian. Your son.'

'You look just like my brother.'

I sit back on the chair, holding Kelya tight, and my heart's racing. The old bugger's lost his marbles now. What the fuck did Kieron do to him? 'Aye, Dad, so people say.'

He winks at us. 'Should see your face, son. Made you think I've got Alzheimer's.'

Dirty old cunt.

'Nothing wrong with you, is there?'

'Everything's wrong with me, son. Everything hurts and I'm a cripple and I need you to get my messages in. But I can still remember what a Hilbert Space is.'

'A Hilbert what?'

'Never mind, son. I've forgotten more mathematics than most people ever learned. I mean, a high school education isn't even the start of the journey.'

Here he fuckin' goes again. Same old story, blah blah fuckin' blah.

There's a shadow at the door and it opens wide. The doctor's standing there, stiff-backed prick. 'Visiting time's almost up, sir.'

'Just a sec.' I give him that knowing nod, that one that says "I'm not taking the piss here, honest" and the boy gives us a smile back, one that says "Cool beans". 'You remember Kelya, Dad?'

'Aye, son. She's bonny. Didn't know you had that much love in you.'

'I've got hidden depths.'

'Maybe you should let people see them every so often?'

'Aye, probably.' I stand up and want to hug the old bugger. But I just nod. 'See you soon, Dad.'

'If you could get us a book next time?'

'Will do.'

'See if there's a new James Patterson out, son.'

'There's always a new James Patterson out. I'll get you some.'

'Thanks, son.'

I give him one last nod, then head out into the corridor, carrying eight months of love and cuddles in my arms. Fuck me, I've got tears in my eyes. Three generations of Bain together. I mean...

'Sir?' The doc is beckoning us into a room.

I take the wee one in and leave the door open. Seen that trick a few times, I tell you. Big office, typical doctor fare. Certificates on the walls, all that jazz.

The doc's behind his desk, prodding his finger off a tablet. He shakes his head and puts it down. 'Mr Bain, I need a word. It's my professional opinion that your father should not be living on his own.'

'I hear you, but what can I do?'

'Can he live with you?'

I hold up Kelya just that wee bit higher. 'Got a young kid, and I can't have him drinking in the house.'

'Ah, yes. His drinking is going to kill him.'

'Is this you saying he's got cancer or something?'

'No. Aside from his motor issues, he's in reasonable health considering his age. I'm more concerned about the *condition* he was in when he was admitted. Drunk as a skunk, as they'd say.'

'Aye.'

'That's it?'

'It's a problem, that's for sure. But I can't put him in a home just now.'

'There are some reasonably priced ones—'

'No, pal, it's not the cost.' I stroke Kelya's perfect wee head. 'It's just, I read this story on the plane back from the States about how care homes are going to be full of the dead and dying.'

'Ah, yes. Covid-19. Well, it's certainly a concern.'

Got a really hard decision to make here. 'Tell you what. As soon as this shite's all over, I'll look at getting him into a decent home. Spare no cost. But until then...' I suck in a deep breath. 'If we can get him off the sauce, he can stay with us. I'll check with the missus, but it should be fine.'

'Excellent.' The boy looks pleased.

Good, because I mean it. 'Need to stop that old bugger getting so pished every day, though. I know it's his only joy left, but he's got to get it under control.'

'Well, it's a challenge and we can offer some support to you.'

'Thanks for looking after him, doctor. He's not easy.'

'Thank you. It's not often we hear such things. I'll let you get back to your day, then.'

I take my time getting to my feet and keep a hold of Kelya as I walk out into the corridor. No sign of Apinya.

Tell you, growing up in Bathgate, it can't have been easy being a Thai lassie with a name like that, but she owns it. Could shorten it to Penny or Pinny or something, but she doesn't want me to. And I'm glad.

Ah, life's good.

I get out my phone to see if she's texted us. Can barely see anything through the glass, but there's a text there. I open it, but it's not from Apinya.

From fuckin' Sundance:
Need a chat with you.
Fuck sake. Way to destroy my good mood. Gloating about his new tenure, no doubt. Prick, prick, prick.
I shoot a message back one-handed:
Just got home. Can we do this tomorrow?
Buzz. *It's urgent.*
What isn't with that arsehole?
Okay, where?
In lockdown. Needs to be on Zoom.
What in the name of fuck is Zoom?

CULLEN

Cullen looked around the kitchen and it was a bomb site. The roasting chicken smelled lovely, and the chilli gravy was a way off thickening. Once it was ready, he'd clean it up, but he just—

That cough hit him hard. Felt like someone was standing on his chest.

Evie smoothed a hand over his back. 'Christ, are you okay?'

'I feel like I'm dying.' Cullen coughed again and it tasted like blood in the back of his throat. 'But I need to do this. Get it out of the way.'

'I'll start peeling those tatties, then.'

'Thanks.' He leaned over to hold her. Kissing was way beyond him just now. And her hands started groping him, running all over his back and stroking and—

His laptop chimed and started playing that annoying ring tone.

Brian Bain calling...

'Let's put that on pause.' Cullen coughed into his elbow. He put his headphones on and clicked Accept.

'Can you hear me?' Black screen, but that was definitely Bain.

'I can hear you.'

'Hellooo?'

'Brian, I can hear you.' Cullen had to check his settings were fine. Bang on.
'Fuck sake. Telling me this was fuckin' urgent and he's—'
'Brian, I can hear you.'
'Oh, right. Hi, Sundance. Oh, that's a nice-looking kitchen there.'
'Wish I could say the same. I can't see you.'
'Right. Just a second.' The black screen shifted to a shot of the one and only Brian Bain, sitting in front of a bookcase filled with fancy cookbooks. He had a week's worth of stubble, all salt and pepper and almost a beard. His lips moved, but nothing came out.
'Brian, I can't hear you now.'
He frowned. His lips moved still, looked like he was saying "fuckin' clown" but Cullen was only guessing. '—me now?'
'That's it.' Cullen leaned forward. 'Thanks for—'
'Eff me, Sundance, you don't look well.'
'I'm not well.' Cullen felt another cough climbing up. He cleared his throat but it didn't do much. 'I've got Covid-19.'
'Bad luck.' He actually looked sympathetic for once. 'Had a bit of a scare with it in the States myself.'
'You okay?'
'Long story, Sundance. But aye, I'm fine. Same with the Boy Wonder.'
'Elvis?'
'You should call him Paul, you know.'
'Okay, so.' Cullen sucked in a deep breath. 'Let's—'
And a pair of bronze arms passed across the screen, then Bain was holding a baby.
'This is my wee lassie, Kelya.'
Whatever traumas Bain had been through with his son, Cullen hoped he'd avoid them with his daughter. Maybe it was easier to fuck up a boy, just let the little shite run wild, but maybe not. Cullen had seen enough tearaways, generations of broken men, breaking the next one by their absence. Or worse, by their presence.
'Say hi to Daddy's boss.' Bain raised her tiny hand and waved at the screen. She giggled and cooed.

And Cullen knew what he was trying to do. He must've known this was coming, and had been coming for a long time. Cullen had been in Bain's orbit a long time. Nine years, give or take. And all that time he'd been cruising for a swift exit. Came close a few times, but he'd somehow scraped free.

'Hear you got a full tenure as DI.'

'I did.'

'Congratulations, Scott. Sincerely. I knew it was coming.'

'Thanks.' Cullen tried clearing his throat again without coughing up a lung. 'No easy way to say this, but I wanted to inform you face-to-face. I'm afraid that, as a result of your unauthorised trip to America, effective immediately, we're demoting you from sergeant to constable.'

Bain sat there, fizzing with energy. He stared down at his daughter, then licked his lips a few times. 'Right.'

'You okay?'

Bain sniffed. 'I'm fine.'

'You know you can't appeal this decision.'

'I know. Had to demote a few numpties in my time.' He stared hard at the screen. 'But I'm not going to apologise.'

'Don't expect you to.' Cullen gave him a kind smile. 'I've fought hard for you to stay on the force. I know there's more to you than this. It was possible you could've been kicked off. Believe me there are those that wanted it. You might've kept your pension, but I thought...'

'I'm not going to thank you.'

'Fine. Look, I know why you did it, Brian. It's understandable, but you broke the rules.'

'Thanks for doing it like this, Scott. I appreciate you doing it like a man. Treating me with respect.' Bain reached an arm forward and Apinya appeared from behind, smiling and stroking the side of her husband's face.

The screen went back to Zoom.

Cullen shut his laptop's lid and sat back in his chair. The fever was melting him like a candle and he was exhausted from that.

Evie was over by the hob, chopping potatoes. The kettle was close to boiling. 'You okay?'

'I've had worse.' Cullen walked over to her, and each step ached. 'But it's done and I can relax now. Maybe get over this thing.'

'Bain was right, you know. You look like shite. Sit down and eat this.' She popped a chunk of carrot in his mouth.

BAIN

The fuckin' screen sits there with Sundance's face plastered on it, frozen in place. Cunt looks ill as fuck. Good.
Would you like to rate this call?
Aye, it was fuckin' pish.
Fuck sake. That total cunt. Who does he think he is? Acting like he's my mate, trying to save us from the mercies of Crystal fuckin' Methven. Who's he think he's kidding? He's wanted me out ever since that first time we met.
Dick.
Total fuckin' dick.
I am not in control here. Fuckin' long way away from being in control.
'Here.' I hold up my wee baby girl to the light of my life.
Apinya takes her, thank fuck. 'You okay?'
'That fudgin' clump demoted us.'
Apinya narrows her eyes. 'Thank you for not swearing in front of Kelya.'
'Right, aye.' I get up and stuff my hands in my pockets. 'Fu — That sneaky fu—' Christ, this isn't easy. 'I can't believe it.'
'Why? This has been in the wind for a long time, hasn't it? It's why Danielle and I suggested you and Paul do that podcast. And it's paying off for you. You've got a long-term plan, Brian.

You've just spent two weeks in America, building things up on the ground. You've got fans and you're good at that show. It's popular.'

'Aye, but podcasts are fu—orked just now. Nobody's buying ads.'

'So go membership only. Or sell out. Whatever, but you've got something going on there. A hundred thousand listeners wanting to hear the latest beer reviews.'

'Maybe.'

'Or you could open a craft brewery of your own. By the time this is all over, you could've perfected the recipe. Maybe even take over the lease of a pub. Sure they'll be cheap enough. Or you could do a podcast about policing. Show the inside of it.'

Oh you fuckin' dancer. That's the fuckin' ticket, that is. Show everyone how much of a bunch of cunts I work with.

'I like that.' I actually laugh. 'What did I do to deserve you?'

'It's more how many mirrors I smashed to deserve you, but I'll take it as a compliment.' She smiles. 'Do you want a beer? Enough boxes came while you were away to keep you in beer until this one's in a care home.' She holds up Kelya high enough to make her giggle.

'That's a bit raw to joke about, love.'

'Oh. Sorry. But do you want a beer?'

'Fu—*or* sure, I'd love one.' I walk over to the beer fridge and see getting one out? I'm spoilt for choice here. A nice hoppy as fudge double IPA. That one from Denver, maybe.

I'm actually thinking of getting some kip. Then again, I'll just be thinking of Scott Cullen all that time.

Fuck sake.

And I'll have to organise the spare room for the old man. It's all stuffed full of Elvis's shite for podcasting, microphones and pop shields and baffle boards on the wall, all the shite he can't fit into his flat, so I'll need to shift that into the garage, won't I?

She puts the beer down on the table along with the bottle opener.

Dad.

'Shite.' I shake my head, trying to dislodge this feeling, but it's in my heart, not my head. 'No, stick it back in the fridge. There's someone I need to see.'

THIS CHAIR'S rock hard on my arse, I tell you. I'm shifting about so much that it's upsetting wee Kelya. Still not anywhere near recovered from that pummelling it took in America and those nuclear painkillers are wearing off.

Still, this video-calling lark is the business.

It's like I'm back in HMP Edinburgh. The number of times I've been in that place to see some stupid wee shite who'd done something bad, only to find that there are a ton of other things said stupid wee shite has done but we haven't busted them for, or that there's some other stupid wee shite who might've done something and they might know something about it…

It's just like I'm sitting across the table from Joey Dowling. 'You lost the moustache, Bri. Have to kick you out of the club.'

'You still waxing yours, aye?'

'Works a treat. Thanks for the tip.'

'Don't mention it, buddy. We should get some beers when this is all over.'

'Sounds ideal.'

There's a knock at the door and I look up. Sounds like it's in this kitchen, but it's not. Christ, this new laptop has fu—abby speakers.

'I'll just get that door.' Dowling shuffles off, leaving us looking at his desk. A pink hand reaches back for a biscuit.

Then a prisoner shuffles in, head slung low, and sits down at the desk. My son, the stupid wee shite jailbird. Looks like someone's gone to town on him, his pus all bruised and covered in plasters where it isn't wrapped in a fuck-off bandage.

'I'll just be here, son.' Sounds like Dowling's chewing. 'You can have one biscuit, okay?'

Kieron can't even look at me.

'Alright, son?'

Still doesn't look at us, just sits there. My idiot son, the bent cop.

Kieron Bain.

Hard as it is to admit, he's my responsibility, my fault. And I've pushed him away, ignored him and left him to fester in there. But he's my flesh and blood, and I owe him a connection at least.

'Alright, Dad.' He looks over at me, finally. And frowns.

'Who's that?'

'This is your sister, Kieron. Your half-sister. Her name's Kelya.'

'Right.' He rubs at his arm and shows us a massive tattoo. And God knows what it's of. Doesn't look too Nazi, at least.

'Nice to see her.' He smirks. 'Another KB name? King Billy. Hear you're the Billy Boy on some podcast?'

'Tried to avoid it this time, son, but Apinya, that's my wife, she wanted to use it. It's her wee sister's name. Died when she was a wean. And she's got her name, not mine. Mine's tarnished.'

'Well. She's cute.'

'Aye, she's going to break hearts when she's older. Much like you did.'

He stares hard at us, and his lips are quivering. 'Dad, I'm sorry. I was a stupid prick.'

'You didn't learn, though, did you?'

'No. Those guards... I didn't want to attack them, but Kenjo... Man, he's brutal. Just went for it, you know?'

'Son, if you testify, you might get a reduced sentence.'

'Right.' He rubs a hand over his stubble. 'I'm weighing it up. It's a murder, right? Grandad's hired this brilliant lawyer, he's going to try and get me off with a lot of it.'

'Right.' I swallow down a heavy lump. 'Kieron, son, it's my turn to apologise for not seeing you inside. What happened hit me hard, have to admit. I blamed everyone, lashed out at people who tried to help. Did myself no favours on that score. But what's worse was I treated you as if you were dead. And the truth is, what happened was my fault. I should've raised you better.'

'No, Dad, you raised me well. Helped me get into the police. I thought I was helping out a mate, but...' He sits back and puts his hands behind his head. 'I wasn't helping anyone. I messed up, Dad, let bad people influence me. I was weak.'

'How you doing in there?'

'Starting to be able to tell the bad from the good.'

'And Kenny Falconer is good?'

'No, but...' He sighs. 'When I heard about Mum, I needed someone's help. Kenjo was the only option. I needed to get out of here and he had a plan.'

'Kenny Falconer, though. What were you thinking?'

'I was desperate.' He tugs at his hair, like he's trying to pull the stubble out by the roots. 'My lawyer reckons, worst case, I'll get another two years for escaping, two for burning Cordell and taking him hostage. If I'm lucky.'

I wait until he looks right at us. 'It might not have been murder, but that prick killed your mother. No regrets, son.'

He nods, slow and hard.

Christ, I wish I was there, in the room with him.

'I heard you got demoted.'

What the fuckin' fuck? 'How'd you hear that?'

'Never mind. Still got my sources.' He scratches at his arm. 'That Cullen guy, wasn't it?'

'Maybe.'

'Dad, I've got a smoking gun against him. I can fuck him over.'

Nothing would give me greater pleasure in this world than seeing Sundance taken down a peg or two.

Time was he was an Acting DC, working for that big lump, Craig Hunter. Now he's a DI. Not even Acting any more.

And I'm sorely tempted to take Kieron up on this, but if there's one thing I've learnt over the years, it's not to take the fruit of the forbidden tree. 'Where did this smoking gun come from?'

'Sure you want to know?'

'Sure.'

'Alan Irvine.'

For fuckin' out loud. I want to smash up the table, hit the wee shite until he sees sense. 'Kieron, for the love of all that's good... The whole reason you're in here is because of that prick. You shouldn't have anything to do with him.'

'It's solid, Dad.'

'I don't care. If I'm going to screw over Scott Cullen, I'm doing it my way.'

~

CULLEN & BAIN WILL RETURN IN

"GORE GLEN"

November 1st 2020

Printed in Great Britain
by Amazon